Number 8

"Keg stand!" someone was  does a keg stand!"

Brothers and others crowde[...] pressed him and he grabbed on to the dented metal edge. He let himself be lifted upside down. . . .

"Yeah, Bret!" someone bellowed by his ear. He took the thick rubber tube in his mouth.

People chanted: "Bret! Bret! Bret!" The music pounded on all around him. *"California knows how to party!"*

Ryan Yeager(meister) pressed the valve and the liquid began to flow, slightly bitter. Liquid poured the wrong way, upward, defying gravity, pulled into his body by the action of throat muscles.

"One . . . ," a cry rose up, "two . . . three . . ."

The flow, its enumeration—this seemed like a beautiful system, a peaceful system that promised some sort of release, some assurance that *what he was doing was right,* and rage and disappointment exploded in Bret's mind as he choked on the liquid and his lungs began to explode at only nineteen.

They quickly set him down and Bret staggered backward. Some fat guy's face loomed up large: "Are you okay, buddy?" Bret nodded and the coughing quickly died. There was a collective breath taken and then . . .

"Yeah, Bret!" probably the same person as before bellowed. His b[...]-ed him. He was [...]nty-one and this [...]

Number 8

someone kept hollering, "Birthday boy ...

... crowd around him. Bodies

...

... the man. He fuckin' kicked ass. He was twent...

... he was legal!

21

JEREMY IVERSEN

Simon Pulse
New York London Toronto Sydney

SIMON PULSE
An imprint of Simon & Schuster Children's Publishing Division
1230 Avenue of the Americas, New York, NY 10020
Text copyright © 2005 by Jeremy Iversen
All rights reserved, including the right of reproduction
in whole or in part in any form.
SIMON PULSE and colophon are registered trademarks
of Simon & Schuster, Inc.
Designed by Sammy Yuen Jr.
The text of this book was set in Trade Gothic.
Manufactured in the United States of America
First Simon Pulse edition March 2005
10 9 8 7 6 5 4 3 2 1
Library of Congress Control Number 2004112066
ISBN 0-689-87623-8

21

What, without asking, hither hurried Whence?
And, without asking, Wither hurried hence!
Another and another Cup to drown
The Memory of this Impertinence!

—Omar Khayyám

Within the armor is the butterfly, and within
the butterfly is—the signal from another star.

—Philip K. Dick

Masters made a promise to Bret. "You are going to get *so* wasted," he said, smashing the squash ball so hard that it streaked back bulletlike at Bret's head. "We're not letting you go to bed until you've had twenty-one units of alcohol."

Bret returned the serve with a flicked wrist. It hit a corner and veered off wildly. Masters dove to catch it. "Units," Bret asked.

"Yeah. Units." Masters tapped the ball lightly upward and Bret prepared an overhand. "Like, one twelve-ounce beer, one glass of wine, one shot—those are units."

Bam! Bret dealt a lazy return. "Thanks, Doctor Pre-Med." He wiped his forehead.

"You're twenty-one, bro. PAK tradition stands." *Bam! Bam!* Sharp sounds echoed around the white-walled chamber. The ball angled off for somewhere else.

1

A crazy angle on the chalkboard. Bret's econ section leader checked her notes and carefully surrounded the angle with three dots. She was a short, bronze-skinned woman from an unknown country where English was never spoken.

"Curve," she said, almost like she wondered herself. Then she nodded. "Emmm . . . economiki . . . is *under. Under* this."

She made a little chirping noise and stood back, pleased.

A girl with curly hair leaned forward in her chair, clutching an exam book. Red ink snaked over the fanned pages. "Wait. Can you say that again?"

"Is *under*," explained the teaching assistant.

The girl tapped her pen and bit her lip.

Bret leaned back in his chair and laid his head against

the wall. A brilliant sunset pressed against the third-floor windows. He stared up at a bright fluorescent light tube. Every now and then the tube flickered.

"Dude, this sucks," Craig whispered to his left.

"Dude, it's my *birthday*," Bret whispered back.

"Oh, shit, that's right!" Craig punched Bret's shoulder softly. The curly-haired girl shot them a wild look. "Happy birthday, man," Craig added a little more quietly.

"Circle," said the TA, drawing one on the board. She never erased the board right, so the circle was almost impossible to see. "Like a rus!" She started giggling.

"What the hell are you doing here?" Craig whispered to Bret. "This is like the first time I've ever seen you in section and it's your birthday."

"I needed to get my test back," whispered Bret.

"Like a rus!" the TA repeated, giggling again. The room was silent because no one had any idea what she was talking about.

"I think she freebases before class," whispered Craig.

The TA drew another line and the chalk screeched.

The curly-haired girl, chin in hand, stared glassily through the blackboard. Her eyes looked like they were watering.

Bret shifted positions. Luck that his birthday coincided with the biggest Pi Alpha Kappa party this quarter. "When's the thing start," he asked.

"I don't know," whispered Craig. "Pretty soon. Drink something."

"Yeah, like what," asked Bret.

Craig unzipped a pouch on his gray Billabong backpack and pulled out a shiny flask. He passed it on low to Bret.

"Hells yeah," whispered Bret. "What is this?"

Craig shrugged.

When the TA turned around and began to dot the circle, Bret took a gulp from the flask.

"My first shot," he whispered, passing back the cold metal. Craig flashed him a *hang loose* sign.

The chalk screeched again. A tear fell onto the curly-haired girl's exam and red ink ran. Beyond the window, palms swayed in the cloud-streaked fire of sunset.

2

Jagged palm-tree edges cut through a purple sky of failing light. Air, not warm or cold, blew through Bret's hair as he longboarded down the Row. A sweep of headlights, a thumping beat, and Bret had to carve to the side of the road as a black truck with big lifts and a Phi Delt sticker tore past.

Lights were on in the houses, but Bret saw through picture windows that guys were just hanging out in the lounges or kitchens or whatever; no one would dare throw a party against them that night. He braked outside the PAK house, kicked up his board, and crossed the wide dark lawn where pledges with sloshing bottles of lamp oil were trying to stake tiki torches in the hard soil. A few burned like orange tears in the twilight.

Bret climbed the stairs and swung open the front door.

Breakbeats pulsed softly from huge speakers around the lounge. By the far fireplace, a DJ with big black headphones slid faders and turned equalizers. Supposedly he was a decent one and played clubs down in L.A.

Bret walked the empty expanse of stain-resistant carpet toward the stairs. The pledges on party prep had hauled all the sofas out. Four black tripods with lights waited motionless and dark in the corners. Dusk hung outside the glass doors that made up the far wall, ceiling lights blazed within.

Marty appeared down the hall hung with composites. "We put *so* much money into this shit, B. Stanton," he announced. "Fuck the dean." Marty was on Social.

"Like how much," asked Bret.

"Lots. We got twelve kegs, hard A, plus some other stuff," said Marty.

"Nice," said Bret.

"And this guy," Marty said, pointing to the DJ. "And uh, jeez, something else . . ."

Bret rested the Sector Nine board on his foot. The heavy plywood squashed his toes. "Dude, you guys went hard core for my birthday," he said.

"Oh, yeah, I heard it was your birthday," said Marty. "Wait, is this—"

"Yeah, twenty-one," said Bret.

"Oh, fuck yeah," said Marty, giving him the snap. His eyes widened: "Aw, this is perfect. You're gonna get mad play."

"Hells yeah," said Bret.

"One more year, bro, one more year," Marty said, punching the wall lightly.

"When're we starting up," asked Bret.

Marty looked at his watch. "Soon." He shrugged.

Bret climbed the stairs to the second floor.

He said "what up" to Briner, who was leaving the bathroom in a towel, and pushed open the cracked wooden door to his double at the end of the hall. It was kinda far from the rest of the house, right above the chapter room. Bret and his roommate Jordan had put a women's restroom sign on the door in the hope that drunk girls would wander in one night. It had actually happened a couple of times but they were *really* trashed, like puking trashed, so the sign just meant bad news.

Heaps of clothes (dirty, clean), papers, old cans (beer, soda), wrappers, and magazines lay on desks and chairs and floorspace and beds, and spilled out of narrow closets and drawers. Jacked road signs covered the walls.

Amid the piles a red light flashed. Bret swept aside crumpled pages and tapped the button:

"Hi, Bret, this is Caitlin from Woodbridge. I, uh, just wanted to call and wish you a happy twenty-first. Okay, I hope everything's going well and you're having fun on your birthday. I'll talk to you later, maybe? Happy birthday. *This message was recorded at—*"

Bret hit the button again.

In sudden silence he stared at himself in the mirror and let his backpack slide onto the floor.

He saw the door's reflection swinging before he even heard it open. Jordan burst through in a suit and a tie with a leather messenger bag slung over his shoulder. "Honey, I'm home," he hollered.

Bret laughed. "Where's my kiss, honey," Jordan demanded.

"Oh, yeah, you want it," Bret said, puckering his lips big and grabbing Jordan.

"Oh, fuck you," said Jordan, breaking out and backing off. He took off the messenger bag and waved the tie. "Yeah, I'm my dad, but you are *definitely* not my mom."

"Yeah, I'm too pretty and I don't sleep around enough," said Bret, and ducked a Nerf football coming at him.

He picked the football off a pile of clothes. Big corporate logo. "So how did the, uh, International Strategic Consulting Group go?"

"ISCG," said Jordan. "Um, I got a football."

"A football and a job," asked Bret.

"A football," said Jordan. He fell down on his bed. "Blow."

"Did you tell the guy you're a PAK," asked Bret, pitching the football up in the air.

"Yeah," said Jordan, rubbing his face with his hands. "But he wasn't."

Bret tossed the football up and down some more. "Well, at least we've got a party," he said.

"Yeah," said Jordan, between his fingers. "I need to drink and I need drugs and I need pooo-tie."

"I need to drink too," said Bret. "I'm only on shot number one."

Jordan stopped rubbing his face and stared at Bret. "Shit, that's right—it's your birthday. We're doing a shot."

He got up and found a handle of bad gin on the floor under a pile of clothes. He poured some into glasses. Jordan toasted: "Happy birthday."

They did the shot.

Jordan gritted his teeth and said, "Ohhh, the pain. Cheers to your last happy birthday."

"Huh," asked Bret.

"Dude," said Jordan. "I don't want to ruin this for you."

"What," asked Bret.

"Well, uh," said Jordan, "your shit gets better and better until twenty-one, right? You know, like you can drive, you can smoke, you can drink. Now think about what happens after that."

Jordan gave Bret two seconds, and then answered. "After two-one it's all downhill. You just get older and you get less cool and people don't let you have fun anymore."

"Oh, bullshit," said Bret.

Jordan sat down on his bed. "I fucking wish," he said. He sloshed the gin around in its bottle. "I wish *I* was a junior again," he mumbled. "I wish *I* was twenty-one again."

"Dude," said Bret. "You're like a year older than me. It's like the same thing."

"No, it's not," snapped Jordan, glaring up at him. "Twenty-two blows. I mean, how the fuck is it better than twenty-one? How is anything ever better than twenty-one? Like, what can you do at forty that you can't do at twenty-one?"

Bret thought. "Rent a car? Uh, be president?"

"Yeah, I'm gonna be president," sneered Jordan. "I can't even be a strategic consuler. Consultant. Whatever. This is the best it gets." He fell back on his bed and pulled off his tie.

Bret's dad took off his tie in the doorway of Bret's room. The striped fabric hung loose in his hand.

"You're applying where," *he asked.*

"Poniente University," said Bret.

"Jesus Christ, Bret, I'm not going to those damn fundraisers for this California bullshit. What Ivies have you got down?"

Bret swallowed but kept his gaze fixed. "I don't have any Ivies down," he said.

His dad walked into the room and Bret pushed his chair a little farther back against the desk.

"You're joking me. Tell me you're fucking joking me."

Bret swallowed again. "No, I don't," he said.

"I went to an Ivy, your uncle and your grandfather went to Ivies. What's wrong with you?"

The heating duct stopped whooshing. In the silence Bret said softly, "Ivies aren't fun."

"Fun? You're picking a college based on fun? What the hell is this, Bret? College isn't about fun." Bret's dad rubbed his face with his hand. "It's about name, it's about opening doors. If we got a résumé that said 'Poniente' at my firm, we'd laugh and chuck it."

Bret didn't say anything. The application pages lay all over his desk.

His dad started back to the door. "And your mother's okay with this," he asked.

"I didn't talk to her yet," said Bret.

His dad looked at him. Then he spat out, "You're gonna throw your life away," and disappeared down the hall.

Bret looked at the application papers and felt sick. He felt like he didn't want to fill out anything at all. Go nowhere.

He swept the white pages into the trash. He had only written his name on the first one. He watched snow drift past the window for a while and then turned on the TV.

Much later Bret woke up to his dad shaking him. "Bret," his dad said. "Hey, Bret. Bret . . ."

Bret smelled alcohol. His dad fumbled for the light switch.

"What, Dad?" groaned Bret.

"Bret, I've been thinking about, about the applying to colleges." Bret's dad looked at the desk. "Yeah, I, uh, think *you should, should go for it. . . ." He saw the papers in the garbage can and he said, "Apply to, uh, Poniente."*

Then he smiled faintly at Bret. His eyes were watery. He held Bret's head and shook it. "Hell, Bret, have fun. Have fun."

"Okay, Dad," said Bret, pulling away.

"Because, Bret . . . ," said his dad.

"Yeah," asked Bret.

"Are you listening to me," asked his dad.

"Yeah," said Bret.

"No, are you really listening," his dad asked.

"Yes," said Bret.

"You won't have the chance ever again."

Bret lay back on his pillow and looked past his father at the ceiling. A red light glowed softly on the smoke alarm.

3

A small red light flared on the balcony and clouds of sweet smoke drifted in. Bret stood in the big triple where Stan Fontaine's stereo pounded and some guys were hanging out.

"Dude, you're fucking with the fabric softener," yelled Fontaine from his futon.

The ceiling lamp was out and blacklights glowed purple, igniting the white stripes across Bret's red T-style polo into bars of light. The Pacific Outfitters shield-patch blazed like an icon on his breast.

"The fabric softener's gay," Wes called in from the balcony. Giggles out there under the first stars of night. The red light glowed again, and another sweet cloud bloomed.

"Fuck, shut the doors or something," said Fontaine.

Bret had showered, changed: board shorts to washed

boot-cut blue jeans, black Reef sandals to chunky brown shoes.

"Are you on this," Wes asked him, holding out the bong.

"No, dude," said Bret. "I'd pass the fuck out. I gotta do the twenty-one."

"Whoa-ohhhhh!" said Wes. "We got a birthday boy!"

"Fuck," said Fontaine, rummaging in a box next to the futon. "We're out of softener." He threw the box, and it bounced off the wall and almost landed in the garbage.

"Nice," said Nick Mengus, who was fixing his hair and saw it in the mirror.

J.P. took the bong. "What number are you on," he asked Bret.

"Like nothing," said Bret. "Two."

"Do I get birthday punches," asked Wes, cracking his knuckles.

"Try it," said Bret, smiling.

Wes bit his lip and went in for a swing, but Bret blocked him no problem. Wes started giggling again and Bret punched him in the shoulder.

"Ouchie," said Wes, rubbing his arm with a mock pained look on his face.

"Any more birthday punches," asked Bret.

"Later," said Wes. "When you're so drunk you can't move."

J.P. tried to blow the smoke off the balcony, but it

wafted back into the room anyway. He winced.

Fontaine didn't even notice, kneeling in front of the fan where he had taped the softener strips. Electric breeze on his face, he moaned, "Thanks for smoking, assholes. You can't even smell it anymore."

Wes took the bong. "It doesn't work, Stan."

"Yeah, it does," said Fontaine. "Like what's the perfect smell for girls, you know? Cologne is sketchy, because they think, 'Oh, this guy's gonna try and hook up.' But fabric softener is clean and fresh, you know, and they're into that."

Over the futon hung a giant purple-and-white tapestry, its intricate patterns burning in the blacklight glow. Bret noticed three axes of symmetry.

Nick Mengus put down his hair paste and pulled open a drawer. "Dude, our room reeks," he said. "Me and Gavin threw your softener shit out yesterday."

Wes cracked up and did the snap with him. "I love you, man," he said and slapped Nick on the shoulder.

"You guys suck," said Fontaine, betrayed. "No one's getting any tonight." He flopped down on the futon and picked up a copy of *The Pony Express*.

"Only *you* need fabric softener to get some," corrected Wes.

The stereo pounded on. Wes lit the bong again.

Nick compared two identical light blue shirts. "I called some girls for pre-party," he said.

Mormon Dave walked past in the hallway and flipped

the light switch on and off, a dazzling flash across the
blacklit room.

A flood of brilliant light poured into the room where Caitlin
paced alone before a stunning backdrop of icy mountain
peaks. Tall, thin, dark hair, flexing her fingers and trying to
breathe in slow, deep breaths.

> *She saw Bret looking in the doorway.*
> *"Did you take one," she asked.*
> *"Huh?" said Bret. "Yeah."*
> *"I'm supposed to feel good," she said, "but I feel all*
like panicky."
> *"That sucks," said Bret.*
> *Darcy was walking along the hall. "A bunch of people*
are in the living room," she told them as she passed. "We're
putting on music and stuff."
> *"Okay," said Bret.*
> *Darcy disappeared around a corner.*
> *"Are you feeling anything," Caitlin asked Bret.*
> *"Nothing yet," said Bret.*
> *He took a step into the room. He could see through the*
window the dark thunderheads that hung over the valleys.
No chance for the slopes today, so people had decided to
stay in this huge cabin and party or whatever.
> *Bret pulled his arm back over his head, stretching.*
"You've got a problem, huh," he asked.
> *"What?" said Caitlin.*

"We've been here for like three days and I've never seen you eat anything," said Bret.

The cabin was above the clouds, though, and up at this height the sun shone brightly on summit icefields.

"I eat things," said Caitlin.

"Okay," said Bret, a little smirk on his face.

Caitlin stopped pacing. "What the fuck?" she cried. Her voice sounded like it was edging up into hysteria. "Why are you like such an expert at watching people eat?"

Bret watched the dazzling play of light on the ice. "I can just tell if somebody has a problem," he said.

"Who the fuck do you think you are," asked Caitlin. She turned to the window.

A pause and then Bret shrugged. He waited for a few moments, watching her back, and then he headed for the door. With his foot on the threshold, for some reason he stopped again.

"Sorry," he said. He didn't say anything else, but he just kinda stood there.

Caitlin didn't move for a while. Then she turned back slowly with her eyes closed. "I feel really panicky," she said in a small voice.

Bret swallowed. "If you just wait," he said, "it goes away."

"What," asked Caitlin.

"Feeling panicky," said Bret.

"Oh," she said.

They stood there. Bret saw Darcy pass in the hall

again, but she didn't say anything and soon was gone.

After a while Caitlin opened her eyes slowly. Her pupils were wide open. "I feel a lot better," she said. A small smile on her lips. "Thanks for hanging around."

A pause. "It's really hard to look good, huh," asked Bret.

For a second Caitlin looked blank. Then shook her head slowly. "I can't believe I'm having this conversation," she said.

"I'm not gonna tell anybody," said Bret. "I was just wondering."

Some kind of bird dipped past the window, glided out toward the distant jagged peaks, a point under the cold, bright sun.

Caitlin sighed. "Okay," she said. "If you knew doing something was wrong, but everybody would compliment you and like you better, would you do it?"

Bret nodded slowly. "Yeah," he said. "Totally."

"Then you've got a problem too," said Caitlin.

Bret opened and closed his mouth but nothing came out. Caitlin smiled.

Just then the Ecstasy hit him and lifted him in a rush. He was projected out and sailing across the expanse too, just standing there and grinning along with Caitlin before that brilliant sun. They ended up talking for a really long time, talking about everything, backlit and frontlit and everywhere lit, his necklace gleaming in that basic light.

○ ○ ○

Bret tucked the chain back under the collar of his shirt. He didn't like it when his necklace hung out.

"Mormon," yelled Stan Fontaine. "I will fucking kill you."

Mormon Dave leaned around the doorframe, smiling, holding a dripping plastic tube. "We almost got the beer bong going," he said.

"Oh, man," laughed Mengus, "that thing's got some nasty shit in it."

Mormon's voice disappearing down the hall: "No, we cleaned it out."

The phone rang and Nick Mengus picked it up and went out on the balcony.

Fontaine tossed the *Pony Express* to Bret. "Haviland's little sister really hates us," he said.

Bret looked down at the newspaper, its pages phosphorescent under blacklight. A picture of a plain girl with a big nose next to a column of text:

The Pen Is Mightier . . .
by Emma Haviland

No Greeks Are Good Greeks!

Like many of my fellow Poniente students, I was elated to learn of the Dean's decision to take away the Alpha Chi Omega Sorority's house last week because of "repeated alcohol violations" while the chapter was already on probation. Like many Ponys, I resent the way a handful of kids trash our campus with their childish antics. What I wonder is: If the Greeks can't grow up, why can't they all go out?

By continuing to allow their irrelevant system to exist, the University is approving of an elitist, misogynistic, patriarchal, racist, and classist institution in a supposed place of education. For many Greeks, binge drinking and sexual assault are regular occurrences.

The immaturity is staggering, and so is—

"This goes on and on, huh," asked Bret.

"That dumb bitch got herself elected to Greek Judicial Panel," Fontaine said. "Haviland needs to put the smackdown on her."

Nick came in from the balcony.

Wes ripped open a case. "Where is Haviland," he asked.

Fontaine shrugged. "I don't think we have info for him."

"Didn't they used to live in town," asked Wes. Fontaine shrugged again.

"The girls are coming," announced Nick. "They're gonna be here like really soon."

"Tight," said Fontaine.

Wes picked up the *Pony Express* and pushed the picture into Bret's face. "Emma Haviland wants you to driiiiiink," he moaned in a witchy voice. "'Drink, Bret, driiiiiiink.'"

"Dude, that's really trippy," said J.P. "You're freaking me out over here."

Wes whirled on J.P. with the *Pony Express*. "Emma Haviland haaaaaates the marijuana," he screeched. J.P. started to fall back in his chair and barely caught himself.

"Tac Pac on Emma Haviland," Bret said.

"Definitely Tac Pac," said Nick Mengus.

"Wait, who are these girls who are coming," asked Wes. "Are we gonna have to Tac Pac on them, too?"

"Some of them are Alpha Phis." Nick shrugged. "I don't know about their friends."

"General Tac Pac for beat-ass bitches," said Fontaine.

"'You are very sexist and bad,'" screeched Wes, and threw the *Pony Express* at Fontaine.

"What's Tac Pac," asked a pledge who was standing out in the hall.

"General Tac Pac for beat-ass bitches," said Bret, and they all put their hands in and made it so.

"It stands for 'Tackle Pact,'" J.P. told the pledge afterward. "You make it when you're sober, so like if any brother gets wasted and starts hitting on a nasty chick, then everybody else has to literally and physically tackle him to the ground."

The pledge laughed. "Nice," he said.

Mormon Dave bust in with the funnel tube. "The beer bong has returned to PAK!" he announced.

"Let's get this shit started," said Fontaine.

"Who's up," asked Mormon Dave.

"Twenty-One is up," said Wes, pointing to Bret.

Bret rolled his shoulders. "Bring it," he said.

"Assume the position," Wes said. He opened a beer and poured it into the funnel while Bret knelt on the rough carpeting and put the plastic tube in his mouth.

The stereo pounded on. Sticky drink rings and the *Pony Express* glowing on the table in front of him.

"A'ight," said Mormon Dave. "Here we go." He tried to turn the valve that connected the funnel to the tube but it stuck. "Oh, fuck," he said.

Then the valve turned and the liquid hit Bret's mouth like a cannon and all he could do was swallow, swallow, swallow so he wouldn't choke.

Bret was choking. The world was rushing, colors drifting and blurry, and Bret on the hard dirt felt fire burning everywhere, in his head, in his body, squeezing lead compression. Sharp spike of pain, spike again, then Bret was spitting out water, streams of water, and Yuri the counselor drove his fist into Bret's stomach again, again, and then Bret gagged, and coughed and gagged and coughed.

He watched the afternoon light shimmer off the lake as he lay wrapped in Yuri's rough towel, shivering and trembling and coughing. Lungs burning, head, nose, throat burning. "I was trying to get there," he managed to say through the pain, pointing to a rock in the middle of the lake with a single tree on it.

"I can't swim that far," Yuri was saying. "You should've listened, Bret. You don't see anyone else swimming out there."

Inside Bret thought he could never freeze and burn so much. Pain.

"Promise you won't do that ever again, okay," Yuri pressed. "You won't take off on your own again, okay?"

"I promise," said Bret. He forced his eyes away from the black tree framed in flashes of golden sun and pulled up the rough warmth of the towel around his knees.

4

Rough carpeting under his knees, last traces of pale liquid sliding down the tube.

The world paused for a second. Bret realized that he was crouching on the floor with an empty plastic hose in his mouth while six people stood watching. Then motion returned.

Wes clapped him on the back. "Nice, Stizanton!" he said. They did the snap. Bret stood up. He felt slightly nauseous, the beer burning in his stomach.

Music pounded. "Who's up next?" yelled Mormon Dave.

"Or is it Stiz*na*nton?" wondered Wes.

"That thing's *sick*," said J.P. "I'm so on it."

Wes was lost in thought. "Stan*tiz*non? Staz to the Anton?" He shrugged.

Mormon Dave pulled a new can from its ring. Chained beers clunked dully on the pitted desk.

Fontaine leaned forward on his futon, its wooden frame creaking. "Don't use up our shit when we've got like ten kegs downstairs."

Nick Mengus examined the tube. Bret felt like the room was crowded and small and he wanted to burst out into bigger space.

"Pledge!" screamed Mormon Dave. "Go get pitchers."

"You really cleaned that thing up," Nick said to Mormon Dave.

"Wait, where are pitchers at," asked the pledge.

"Yeah, it took like forever," said Mormon Dave.

"There're some in the barroom on the shelf under the bar," Fontaine told the pledge.

Bret's roommate Jordan walked by the door, and Bret smiled and flashed a *hang loose* sign.

"Wait, what shelf," asked the pledge.

"Dude, it's right under the bar," Fontaine told the pledge. "Don't trip over the fucking Source while you're at it."

The pledge froze. None of the pledges knew what the Source was, but it filled their lives with mortal terror. It was somewhere in the house. Touching it by mistake meant instant expulsion.

"I thought the cabinet was locked," mumbled the pledge.

"Well un-fucking-lock it," said Fontaine.

A faint breeze blew in from the open balcony doors.

Bret smelled distant desert vastness, sensed a crackling of tumbleweed and scorpions and darkness beyond the valley where miles of tract housing and strip malls rolled on under a blue-black sky.

"Fuck, I'll get the pitchers," said Bret.

"Thanks, Staznanton," said Wes, clapping loudly over the heavy beat.

The music was thudding somewhere outside; Bret didn't put his radio on when he came here. He drove his Jeep fast, doors locked, cover fastened down.

He never knew who he was supposed to be when he passed the county line. This world felt unreal, not a true place, a type of dreamscape in permanent disconnect from the rest of his life.

He swerved around a gray bag with trash spilling out that someone had kicked into the street. The tattered plastic shone in the sun. Then he hit his brakes hard because a guy with a sideways cap and a big Rocawear shirt had wandered into the road. The guy took his time crossing and trailed his fingers across Bret's hood and squinted in at him.

Overflowing garbage cans waited on a square of parched and patchy grass outside the light blue house where Bret parked. He hooked The Club onto his wheel and stood in front of a white door with SIXTY-FOUR written over it in heavy black marker. The smell of onions cooking, a distant woman's voice screaming in Spanish.

The buzzer hung down on wires, so he knocked on the door. Voice from inside: "'S open."

The living room was small and dark and only a little light seeped around the window curtains. Tyrell Jr. lay on the sofa watching Terminator 2 on a big TV. He weighed about three hundred pounds and didn't get up much and wanted to play pro football one day.

"Shantarra's here, right," asked Bret.

Tyrell Jr. sucked on his Big Gulp Coke and the straw made a slurping sound in the ice. "She in the room," he said, barely glancing at Bret.

In the short back hallway Bret squeezed past a row of shopping bags stuffed with clothes and old toys and a mirror frame and newspapers. The door was open.

"Hey," said Bret.

Shantarra was sitting on her bed. She had a purple pen and was drawing her name in puffy, graffiti-style writing on the front of her binder.

"Hi, Bret," she said, putting a curved triangle in an A.

A pop CD was playing in the radio on the chipped dresser between her bed and Tyrell Jr.'s bed, not loud, not soft. "You gonna look at my homework," she asked.

"Yeah," said Bret. "How do you think it went?"

Shantarra shrugged. Bret picked the textbook off her bed. She had pictures of singers she'd cut from magazines taped on the wall.

She started another triangle. "I never asked you," she said. "You getting paid to do this?"

"I wish," Bret said, smiling. "It's something the guys in my fraternity do."

"Y'all are all doing this," asked Shantarra.

"No, not everybody," said Bret. "But everyone's supposed to do an hour a week."

"You're here more than an hour, sometimes," said Shantarra, shading the triangle.

The door to the house slammed. "Jesus!" wheezed a voice.

Bret thought. "I guess," he said.

"When I had my test last week, you came by twice," said Shantarra.

"Uh, yeah," said Bret.

"I got the Kraft macaronis in the bag here," the voice shouted.

Shantarra cocked her head at him. Her braids fell to one side. "Why you care so much," she asked.

Bret looked out the window at the house next door. He would be able to see right in except their window had broken and they had covered it with a pink shower curtain with little flowers on it. "Well, uh, you're really pretty good at math, and you definitely have a good shot at getting into Carver."

Shantarra just looked at him.

"I mean, that's what you said you wanted to do, right," asked Bret.

"Why ain't you answering me?" bellowed the voice from the hall.

"I hear you, Grandma," yelled Shantarra. "Thank you." She kept looking at Bret.

"Right," asked Bret.

Outside a car clattered past. Shantarra shrugged.

Bret opened up the textbook. He found her notebook sheet, wedged between the pages. Her name, the date, eighth grade, teacher's name. The rest of the sheet was blank. He even turned it over, just in case.

Bret felt lightheaded. "Where are the problems," he asked, softly.

Shantarra twisted a braid. "Some kids are makin' fun of me," she said.

Bret closed his eyes. Vertigo. He couldn't stand to be here but he had to be here.

"They say I'm trying to be white," said Shantarra.

"Who," he asked, calm through the struggle to breathe. Everything was unraveling, but this time he would hold it together with his own hands.

Bret's fingers gripped the worn banister as he went down the stairs. With the ceiling lights off, the lounge felt big and empty. The DJ was spinning seamless house off real vinyl, and in the corner Marty was talking to a couple of hired security guys in shiny sapphire jackets.

Bret walked across the open floor and felt levels of

music and layers of rhythm filling space around him; rising and falling pockets swirled through a suspension in air. The sound muffled as he turned off into the short hall to the barroom.

Here the lights were still on. They shone dully on a white linoleum floor waiting to become sticky. The Pi Alpha Kappa coat of arms loomed over a big wood counter: a yellow torch on a green shield surrounded by stars.

Social Chair Kevin Whalen stood behind the counter. He had lined up five colored plastic cups. Pledges were watching him.

"Bar duty is like sacred," Kevin was saying. "You control the party. You guys control the party."

Bret walked around the pledges.

"Okay, so cups are five bucks. But you guys are gonna make the very key call about which cup you're giving."

Bret ducked behind the counter. "What's up, Stanton," Kevin asked.

"I'm looking for pitchers," said Bret.

"Shit, there should be some down there," said Kevin.

"Right on," said Bret, and opened cabinet doors.

"Okay," said Kevin. "Priority cup system for tonight. Remember this, remember this, remember this. This is really key. What are you going to do?" He pointed at a pledge.

"Remember this," said the pledge.

It was really dark in the cabinets, and there was lots of random stuff down there.

"Oh, yeah," said Kevin. He picked the first cup, a red one. "Okay, red cup. This time I've got red cup as top priority. You're giving this to brothers and really hot chicks you want to get *shithoused*. If you see a red cup, you serve it first."

Kevin waved the cup around. "Red cup. Top priority. A'ight?"

Bret pulled out something he thought was a pitcher, but it was actually another beer bong.

Kevin grabbed the blue cup. "Okay, blue cup. This time it's like second best. You give the blue cup to our friends who aren't brothers and to pretty good-looking girls. Serve the red cups first, then the blue cups. Okay?"

Pledges nodded.

Bret pulled out the dog's old bowl. They used to have a house dog but it died. It spent hours chasing its tail and wore a bandanna around its neck. When it died, the guys who liked it were sad.

Kevin held up a green cup. "The green cup is gonna be our average cup tonight. Decent-looking girls and guys we kinda know. You're going to give most people green cups."

Bret found a plastic pitcher, kind of dirty, and put it on the floor.

Kevin picked up a yellow cup. "Yellow cups are not so good," he said. "Give these to girls we don't want drinking much in case they decide to rape us, and dorks we don't really want here. By the time you're done serving the red, blue, and green, most are just gonna give up, and that's a good thing."

Bret found another pitcher and stood.

Kevin pointed at the final cup, a clear cup. "I'm not even going to touch that one," he said. "It's like touching the Source. The clear one is for heinous beastie fat girls and guys who wandered in from the Tech Quad."

Bret rinsed out his pitchers in the sink behind the bar. Cold water splashed down from the high spigot and pinged in the metal basin.

"Do not serve the clear cup! I don't care what happens, if she's the only girl waiting, you're still not serving her. Say you're out of beer, fake a seizure, I don't care what you do. Don't serve the clear cup!"

The keg was iced in a red bucket. Bret emptied foam from the black tube and watched it dissolve on the bed of ice. He started to fill a pitcher.

"Obviously, don't tell anyone what tonight's cup system is because they'll want to kick our asses. Next party, we scramble it up. Except the clear cup, which is always the clear cup. Okay?"

The pledges nodded.

"Okay, Chris?" said Kevin.

One of the pledges nodded again.

Bret had filled up the first pitcher. He put it on the counter and started the second.

"Pop quiz, Chris," said Kevin. "Someone shows up with a clear cup. Who are they?"

Chris smiled. "They're, uh, a beastie fat chick or a lost guy from the Tech Quad."

"Do you serve them, Chris," asked Kevin.

"No," said Chris. "No."

"Do we serve the clear cup," Kevin asked the group.

"No, we don't serve the clear cup," he helped the pledges to chorus.

Bret turned around. "If you serve the clear cup, Stanton will kick your ass," Kevin said.

"Hells yeah," said Bret. Liquid lapped against the plastic as he took a pitcher in each hand and left. The barroom duty list was captured on corkboard, ballpoint names pinned by the door.

Only a corkboard broke the thin white walls of this small office. Computer on the desk, screen turned away from Bret. A dumpy middle-aged woman poked at the keyboard. Big red-framed glasses under a pile of curly blond hair.

"Well, okay there, Bret," she said, looking at the monitor. Painful Minnesota accent.

Bret played with his backpack strap and waited.

She turned and smiled at him. According to the gold plate on her desk, she was PATTY C. COWELL, ADVISING ASSOCIATE. "So what do you want me to putcha down for, Bret," she asked.

"I'm not sure," said Bret.

"You're not sure?" she repeated, mouth an O. "Well, Bret, what area are you interested in?"

"I'm kinda interested in a lot of stuff," said Bret, shifting in the chair.

Patty Cowell's smile got bigger. "Okay. Okay! So we're just gonna have to narrow you down here, Bret." She moved her hands together for a visual, something broad becoming something small.

"Could I maybe have some more time," Bret asked, words catching.

Patty Cowell shook her head. "No, Bret, you really can't," she said. "We really want you to have a major declaration by the end of freshman year. We're not jokin' about that." She tittered.

Bret looked desperately around the room. Cowell had covered the corkboard with inspirational quotes and snapshots of her children.

"So tell me, Bret," she said. "Are you a business-y person? A science-y person? An artsy kinda person? Who are you?"

Bret started bouncing his foot. "I'm not really sure," he said. "I, uh, I wish I had a little longer."

"I've gotcher form open here, Bret," Patty Cowell said, a little sternly. "You had plenty of time to talk over your choices with Melissa. Have you been meeting with Melissa?"

Melissa was his first-year peer adviser. She was a junior and she had thrown up in the hot tub during "Rodeo," wearing only a fringe skirt and cowgirl hat. She had the blue cup, which was bad then, and was kinda chunky and funky, but a beer-goggled Carl Corday had hooked up with her because there was nobody around to pull the saving Tac Pac.

"Yeah," said Bret.

"Well, good!" said Patty. She leaned forward a little in her chair and stared at him, smiling expectantly.

A long pause.

"It's just a really big choice," pleaded Bret. "I could see doing a lot of stuff, maybe."

"That's why I'm here to help you narrow yourself down," Patty Cowell assured. "'Education is specialization.'" She pointed proudly to a handmade piece of calligraphy on her corkboard. Little flourishes of violet ink.

"Oh," said Bret.

"But don'tcher worry, Bret," said Patty Cowell. "I'm gonna be your guide through the process here."

"Thanks," said Bret.

"So for example, do you like business, Bret," she asked. Her big red glasses made her eyes look huge.

"Yeah, I guess," said Bret.

Patty Cowell beamed and slid her chair over to the computer. "Wonderful!" she said. "So should I put that in? Business?"

Bret froze. "Uh . . ."

Suddenly Patty was testy, snappish. Her ginormous eyes fluttered. "Bret, you've put this off to the end of the year and I need to have something down on your form."

"Okay," murmured Bret.

She nodded and typed the word in slowly with two index fingers. He heard her clunk away all eight letters and hit enter. Sharp report with deep echoes like a vault door slamming. Bret's stomach lurched.

Patty turned to face him and a second later her big eyes followed. "Now, that wasn't so painful, was it, Bret?" she laughed.

Bret smiled a little and absently drummed his fingers. There were lots of things he was trying not to think about.

"Now, this time next year—and hopefully a little earlier, Bret—I'm going to want to see you back in here to declare your primary concentration, yeah."

"Uh-huh," Bret said faintly. A copier outside the open door began to whir and pump out white pages.

Patty turned back to the computer. "Great, so we'll just lock you out of non-business classes here, Bret, and getcher on your way then."

"What," asked Bret, slowly.

"We discourage students from cross-registering for classes in other schools, Bret." Patty Cowell tapped a few keys and smiled again.

"Wait, so I can only take classes in the School of

Business," Bret asked. He glanced over and saw the copier light flash under its heavy tan lid. Smell of toner.

"You can take a full range of business-related, department-approved electives, Bret. Your department office has the list of approved electives."

"What if I want to take something that's not on the list," Bret asked, voice breaking a little.

Cowell mused. "I believe we have petition forms here," she said. "Somewhere." She leaned forward and winked one huge eye. "Honestly, though, Bret, they don't usually get approved. We discourage students from cross-registering for classes in other schools."

Bret stared at the desk. Cold coffee rings around a cup where Ziggy clutched heart balloons. He felt like many things were shattering, very old buildings collapsing.

Cowell watched his face. "I'll tell you what, Bret," she said after a while. "It's kinda bending the rules a bit."

Bret looked up. "Yeah," he asked.

"This form goes into the system in two weeks. If you want to change anything, just give me a call before then, okay?"

Her desk phone started to ring. "Thank you," said Bret.

"My pleasure, Bret," Patty Cowell said, and smiled. "We want everyone to be happy." She half-rose to shake hands and smooth down her plaid skirt. Before she picked up the phone, she gave him her card.

○ ○ ○

Noah took the guard's time card and looked it over blankly. Sound filled the huge lounge, and the windows were wrapped by full night. Both Noah and Marty were talking to the security guys, DJ aloof in the light of his mixing board, cocooned in headphones.

"Yeah, maybe like six hundred," Marty was saying as Bret passed him on the way to the stairs. The guards were Mexican and their faces were blank.

Bret climbed, careful not to spill any beer, and at the halfway point where the stairs turned he ran into Masters.

"Bret Stanton, the man himself," said Masters.

"What up," said Bret.

"How's the twenty-one going," asked Masters. He leaned on the wood banister post.

"Not so great," said Bret. The dark wood polish had worn away on the post where generations of PAKs had rubbed against it.

"How many," asked Masters.

"Uh, like three," said Bret.

"Are you joking, Bret," asked Masters. "You're really slacking." He cracked his neck.

"Yeah, I had like section late," said Bret.

"Dude, fuck section," said Masters. "This is like major PAK tradition. Everybody does the twenty-one."

"I'm doing it," said Bret. The pitchers were getting heavy. Bret shifted his grip.

Masters smiled. "You gonna pound those," he asked.

Bret laughed. "This is refills. Mormon got the beer bong going again and I did one."

"Dude, why are you hauling pitchers," asked Masters. "A pledge should be doing that."

Noah jogged up past them ("sorry") and the stairs creaked. Bret shrugged. "I don't know," he said.

"Weren't there any pledges around," asked Masters.

Bret shifted his grip on the pitchers again. They looked kinda green under the dim energy-saving bulb the university made PAK install.

"The pledges shouldn't see juniors getting pitchers," said Masters. "They have to know it's their job."

Bret heard voices up on the second floor. A thin crack snaked up the landing wall through chipped paint. "My bad," he said.

Masters looked at him for a little while. "No worries, bro." He smiled. "So I guess you're gonna chug right now."

Bret raised a pitcher. "One of these," he asked.

"Yeah, at least a unit," said Masters. "I'll tell you when."

Bret held the pitcher up and began to drink. He realized he could see the crack on the wall through the plastic. Music was pounding downstairs and there was laughter upstairs, and he kept drinking as fast as he could.

"Okay, that's one," said Masters at last.

Bret shook himself. "Ahhh," he said, and smacked his lips.

Masters clapped a hand on Bret's shoulder. "Right on," he said. "That's the way to happiness."

A few steps later, he added, "Now hurry the fuck up or you won't have time for twenty-one."

Bret brushed back against a poster about Study Abroad and it fell down.

Bret pulled the solar system poster off his wall, folded it up, and put it in the big box. The poster almost didn't fit because the box was already crammed with a bunch of stuff from his desk, but Bret managed to tape the cardboard flaps down anyway.

Now the room was empty except for him and the box. Four bare white walls, a sunny morning window, and the high vent blowing air conditioning. He wondered how far he could go away from this point.

Bret bent his knees, hauled the box up into his arms, and walked out the door, shutting it behind him with his elbow, plunging the long hallway into shadows.

Dark wooden floorboards squeaked underfoot, a faint smell of old wood and lemon polish. Martina waited in a doorway for him to pass. She pulled off her yellow rubber gloves. "Good," she said. "Your room finish now?"

"Yeah," said Bret.

The steps groaned on his way down. At the bottom he rested the box on a low cutaway wall. The living room was bare except for bright morning sunshine and stacks and stacks of identical boxes with precise white labels. The closest one was SILVERWARE II.

The front door clunked open and a mover came in. He smelled like cigarette smoke and wore a blue shirt with sweat stains under the arms. He saw Bret leaning on the box. "Need help with that, chief," he asked.

"No thanks," said Bret.

"All right," said the guy, going down the hall into the dining room where the other movers were taking apart a big table.

Bret scooped up the box again and walked toward the entranceway. It was really hot and humid outside, even so early in the day. Bret squinted against the sunlight as mosquitoes buzzed around his head. He walked down the front path to the curb where the big orange moving truck was parked. The back was open, little ramp leading up to a dark inside where dim shades of boxes towered.

Bret turned and dropped his cardboard box in front of the blue garbage bin. Kneeling amid circling bees, he pulled a black marker from his pocket and scrawled TRASH across the top.

5

This really pale girl was trying to make out the black numbers she had scrawled on her crumpled sheet of note-book paper. "Excuse me," she called to Bret, giggling. "Do you know where Nick Mengus's room is?"

Her friends moved slowly down the hallway, peering at doors. Lots of long blond hair, pastel tops, short black skirts, heels. Some of them had definitely pre-partied before the pre-party.

"Yeah," said Bret, holding up the pitchers. "I'm going there."

"Oh, good," said the girl. "We'll just follow you."

"Don't mind us," said another girl. They all giggled and headed down the hall with Bret.

"No worries," said Bret. "Yeah, we're just having some beers and stuff."

"There're some people downstairs," said one of the girls.

"Yeah," asked Bret.

"Uh-huh," said the girl. "Not like a lot of people, but some people."

"Yeah, we're going down soon," said Bret.

Then they were all in the big blacklit triple and everyone was chilling and Fontaine had the music turned up. Mormon Dave poured part of a pitcher into the top of the beer bong.

"Are you really Mormon," a girl asked him.

"No," he laughed.

Bret heard them somewhere behind his back because he was talking to another girl. She looked exactly like all the other girls except her hair was light brown and not blond.

The balcony door banged shut. "Are you going to smoke," Bret asked the girl.

"Like smoke cigarettes or *smoke* smoke," asked the girl.

"Like smoke out," said Bret.

"Oh my God," said the girl. "You're a 'smoke out' person! Like I just don't understand why 'smoke up' people say that. I mean, up *where*?"

Because of bizarre and forgotten accidents of history, America divided geographically into regions where people used either one term or the other to refer to smoking marijuana. Bret had seen drunk guys at parties punch each other over which expression was right.

"Yeah, seriously," said Bret, rubbing his chest.

"That's so cool," the girl said. "Like most people here are 'smoke out' people. Are you from here?"

Bret laughed. "No, I'm, uh, from Massachusetts." Lots of voices out in the hall.

The girl stared at him for a second. "Oh, wow," she said. "Did you have like culture shock coming to So Cal? You totally seem like you're from here."

"No," said Bret. He shrugged. "I just paid attention."

"That's cool," the girl said distantly. She was turning around the room. "Wait, what's the theme of this party," she asked.

Bret looked out the balcony window at the palms. Behind them on distant mountains glittered an unworldly skeleton, the huge parabolic dish of the National Observatory. Bret's eyes snapped back to the girl. "No theme," he said. "Just a party."

"Wait, but don't you guys always have like themes for your parties, like 'Rodeo' and, uh, 'Mardi Gras'?"

"Yeah," said Bret. "Uh, this actually used to be 'Run for the Border.' It was like Mexican style and kinda tied into spring break."

"So why aren't you guys like all Mexican and stuff," the girl asked, finger on her lips.

"MEChA and shit protested last year and the dean said we couldn't do the theme this time," Bret said.

"Oh my God," said the girl, "you've got to be kidding. You're such a liar."

"No," said Bret. "I wish."

"Then that is *so* booty," the girl wailed. "That's like . . . Booty Booty McBooty." She hovered on the verge of tears.

Three of the girls started yelling, "Alpha Phi in the house!" Arms around one another's shoulders, holding up their drinks.

"We will do *anything* for money," one of them was saying.

"Oh my God, they are *so* wasted," Bret's girl said, rolling her eyes.

"Hook up with each other," Fontaine suggested.

"Yeah, let's see that," said Wes.

"How much," asked one of the girls.

"We totally need Tracy!" another girl cried, and started to pull on the girl Bret was talking to.

"Hello?" said Tracy, pulling back. "I have mono?"

They tussled and the other girl gave up. "You are being *so* No Fun Allowed," she sulked.

"How much will you give us to hook up with each other?" another girl repeated.

"Five bucks," said Fontaine.

"Ten bucks," said Jordan, who had wandered in with a big crew of other people. The room was getting loud, the music upstairs, downstairs, pounding.

"That's *it*?" said the girl.

"Well, what do you mean by 'hook up,'" asked Mormon Dave. "Like we're talking the kiss, some groping here?"

"Yeah, you'll just see," said one of the girls.

"We got ten and ten here," said Wes, handing over the bills. "Twenty. Go nuts."

"Whatever," said the girl. She finished her drink and banged the glass down on a table. "Alpha Phi in the house!"

The music was surging and a lot of people had crowded the room and spilled out into the hall. Voices rising, sound rising, signaling more bodies pouring into the big area downstairs, filling the barroom and the backyard and the hallways and stairways of Pi Alpha Kappa. Through the swelling din the three girls grabbed one another's shoulders and pulled into a big, sloppy three-way kiss in the middle of their tight circle and then slid their hands down the backs of one another's pastel tops.

The guys were screaming. Bret was yelling too, shouting, "I'm gonna drink to this shit," and he pulled a beer out of Fontaine's case and pounded it in four seconds.

The party started. Imperceptibly, a hidden tipping-point clicked over.

The bolt clicked as Bret fumbled with his key in the lock. He swung the door open. It bumped against a laundry bag, shuddered, and rebounded a little. Little wisps of cotton fell off the ridiculous name sign the resident assistants had put up. Hallway light sliced into the darkness and Sanjay shifted under the covers in a rustling of sheets.

"Sorry, Sanjay," Bret whispered loudly.

Bret shut the door and dumped his Nike duffel bag on the bed. He stumbled over a hamper and crunched a crinkly packet of ramen on the floor before he made it to his desk and switched the small lamp on. Sanjay flopped around his bed again.

Bret hit the trackpad on his laptop and opened up e-mail. A new messages chime thundered out of his speakers, splitting the night. Sanjay flailed.

"Sorry, Sanjay," Bret whispered, and turned the volume knob down.

A lot of the messages were old "Big Sur camping retreat BE ON TIME" shit that he hadn't checked before they left, and three copies of something called "Advisee Appointment Scheduling." But there in the middle: something different.

Bret tapped down to it.

To: Bret Anthony Stanton ‹bboy@poniente.edu›
From: Caitlin Sophie Taglauer ‹ctaglauer@umichigan.edu›
Subject: Hey

Hi Bret! This is Caitlin from Woodbridge, I hope you remember me. :-)

Anyway I rememebred that you are a Pony down there in southern California and I just wanted to write and say what's up! I'm actually going to be by your school on our spring break (yeah semesters) in a couple of weeks because I'm helping my grandma move down to Santa Barbera.

If you're around it would be fun to catch up and all that good stuff . . . even if your not write me sometime because I totally want to know how everything's going, ok? C
PS. DO you have IM?

"Shit," said Bret. He looked at scuffed paint on the cinderblock wall. Then he got up and coughed and stepped on the ramen again and unzipped his Nike bag.

Suddenly Sanjay leaped from bed in his T-shirt and boxers. He stormed out of the room, slamming the door.

Bret just stood there in the dark, holding a pair of ankle socks. "Geez, Sanjay," he called at door. "What the fuck. Chill out." Some actives had warned him the guy sucked after he yelled at them during a roll-out.

The room was silent and dark except for the glow of Bret's laptop. Dirty concrete walls sealed him in, heavy, suffocating, dense, unmoving. Bret had to get the hell out of the Towers. He swung a hand past his face just to watch motion.

6

Something arced past Bret's face from maybe the balcony above, a crumpled-up red flyer of the kind plastered across campus. Body text: PAK BLOWOUT!!! Graphic design: a picture of John Belushi from *Animal House* spewing chunks.

Bret lounged by the doorway of the house with his brothers and watched the crowds pushing to get in. Shiny-jacketed security strongly enforced the invites-only rule. Colored lights strobed inside behind the windows. A pulsing electronic beat rolled out into the night. Some random guys were screaming off the balcony.

Masters pushed his way out through the stream of people and put a heavy hand on Bret's shoulder. "How many is it so far?" He grinned.

"Umm, I'm on five," said Bret. "I've got a little buzz going."

Masters shook his head. "It's late, bro. You've got to represent better than that."

Bret smiled and gave him the snap. "Yeah, I know." He pushed his way back inside through the crushed-up people clutching manila invite cards printed with PAK.

A fight broke out at the door. Some drunk guy screamed "Fuck you all!" and got thrown hard into the bushes. The security guys looked worried and then they laughed.

Laughter from the barroom, where Nate and K-Money had advanced to the final round of their own broom and mop combat tournament. The volley of clacking sticks echoed around the empty common room like gunshots as Bret picked up crushed colored cups and Hawaiian leis and tossed them into a big black garbage bag.

He had taken a few solid hits off Mike Michalek's four-foot bong and he hummed along to the "Savings Is Real at FreshChoice" jingle playing on a boombox in the corner. He smiled when one cracked green cup on the mantelpiece spilled cold beer over his fingers.

As hazy dawn sky lightened outside the big glass windows, he turned to see the front door to the house open slowly.

"Hey, Masters!" said Bret.

Masters startled and then he smiled. "Bret Stanton, my Little Bro!" He headed for the stairs. "Be proud to be cleaning up for your fraternity. Are you proud?"

"Dude," said Bret. "What the fuck happened to you?"

Masters had a really flushed face and his hair was messed up.

"This," said Masters, "was a wild fucking night!"

"Hells yeah!" said Bret. "Everybody . . . got lei'd!" He couldn't help smiling again and Masters was beaming too. "You got lei'd," announced Bret.

"Yes, I did," said Masters, on the first step.

"And you got into a fight," said Bret.

"Huh," asked Masters.

Bret pointed to a red streak on Masters's Hawaiian shirt.

Masters looked down. The clacks echoed around the room. "Yeah, sorta." He grinned. "Good night, kid."

"Good night, Masters," said Bret.

Then he was alone again with the rising sun and mountains of cups to be trashed. A kickass song came on the radio and he turned the volume way up.

Damn, the sound was loud. Props to the DJ. Had they actually managed to find a good one?

Bret had his own great find, a freshwoman he had spotted waiting in the barroom line. He had a pledge hook her up with a red cup and got her served before anyone else.

Now warm gratitude touched her wide blue eyes. "So, do you live here," she asked. Blond hair, tight white shirt. First-years were by definition easy for fraternity guys, especially for upperclassmen like Bret.

"Yeah," he said. They stood off to the side. The green-cup masses envied them. He beamed down with his best white-toothed, dazzling smile.

"Wow. What's that like? It must be amazing."

"Oh, yeah! This is really a great group of guys. They're crazy."

The girl laughed nervously and adjusted her bra strap. "My friend Melanie was kind of going out with a frat guy but like not really. I think it was some guy from Teke." She gulped some beer.

There was a pause. "What are you, um, studying," she asked.

"Business," said Bret.

The girl thought about it. "Yeah, wow. I don't know what I'm doing yet."

Bret nodded solemnly. He took a breath and put his hands on her shoulders. "I'm twenty-one today," he said. "It's my birthday."

She gazed up at him. Eye contact. The electronic music, loud as God, cycled endlessly through the same four tones as colored lights tracked up and down the DJ's console.

Then they were dancing, somewhere in the center of the huge mass of bodies, dancing in a darkness lit by swirling colored lights projected from four corner tripods. The lights spun around them, swinging to the insistent everywhere-beat that overrode all other things.

Bret bounced along to the beat and put his arms behind the white-shirt girl's back. The girl moved forward a little and they were pressing against each other, dancing together to the music that thundered and commanded everything. You couldn't think when it was playing like that, but you could see and feel.

Now he had his hands on the girl's ass, and they were moving side to side together. He looked down at her with the right smug smile. Her eyes flicked up and she smiled too. Bennett had gotten a hand job on the dance floor from a frosh like a couple weeks ago. Maybe he'd get lucky too.

The tones rose and the tones fell. Around the edge of the room there was space to circulate, and in that space hundreds of people passed to and from the barroom holding red and blue and green and yellow cups. They crossed past Bret as he danced, the same faces swinging back and forth in circular motion, orbiting the center where he danced with a girl who had just slipped her hand into his back pocket.

Bret put the paper back in his pocket. He was five minutes late.

Rice Quad lay at the center of campus, a broad stretch of grass surrounded by the massive columned buildings of the School of Humanities and Social Sciences. Clusters of palms dotted the grass and concrete paths crossed it, and among the dots and crosses guys played Ultimate barefoot and girls lay out to tan on bright towels.

All paths converged on a giant ornamental fountain in the middle of the grass. It tossed pillars of spray high into space, forming a prism for light that drew vivid rainbows in misty air. Bret made his way toward this center through students walking, biking, skating, blading to and from class.

A girl with a shaved head and a very bright smile tried to give him a pamphlet.

A couple of guys in black T-shirts doing some obnoxious improv tried to sell him tickets to a Pony Playhouse Presents . . . musical.

A guy with a girl in headscarf played Lebanese music on a boombox and tried to make him aware of Islamic Awareness Week.

Then Bret arrived at the much abused statue of university founder Harold Merton right in front of the fountain. He breathed in, out. There a tall girl waited for him in shade. He swallowed.

"Hey, Caitlin," he said.

Caitlin smiled. "Hey, Bret," she said. She hugged him and he hugged her back.

"So how do you like Poniente," he asked.

Caitlin looked around. "It's really different," she said. "Definitely a lot warmer than I'm used to, but that's probably a good thing." She actually looked really good. She had on sunglasses and her hair was down and she was thin and she was wearing cutoff low-riding denim shorts.

"So you want to get lunch or something," asked Bret.

"Sure," said Caitlin.

They started walking.

"So, how do you like it here," she said.

A couple of guys tried to get donations to race a solar car.

A man with a megaphone yelled at them that Jesus was their personal savior, and tried to give them tiny bibles.

"Well, these people are annoying," said Bret.

"Yeah," Caitlin said, and laughed. "We have them up at Michigan too. I think they really believe students care about things and are into ideas."

"I sure don't," said Bret. "I don't know anyone who's into that stuff."

Caitlin was looking all around. "Actually, I don't really either. They're mainly into partying and getting jobs." She blinked. "It's kinda sad, actually."

Bret shrugged. They cut out across the grass. The blades wrapped around Bret's sandals and tickled his feet.

"So what are you into these days," asked Caitlin.

Bret thought. "Mainly partying," he said with a smile. "I haven't gotten to the jobs part yet, but I go to class sometimes."

"Are classes interesting," asked Caitlin.

"Not really," said Bret. Bright sunlight even through his glasses, commotion of voices around them.

"Well, you've got that famous, uh, observatory," said Caitlin. "Have you ever checked that out?"

"No," said Bret. "Why would I?"

"Well," said Caitlin. She shrugged. "I thought you might be interested or something."

"I'm a business major," said Bret. "We don't have anything to do with that stuff."

"Oh," said Caitlin.

They came to a folding table with duct tape around the part that folded. There four bleached-blond guys in green shirts concentrated on slicing fish and wetting seaweed. A big sign commanded: SUPPORT PUNISHERS WATER POLO! BUY SUSHI!

Caitlin stopped to watch.

"Hey," said Bret. "I heard about this. Like the water polo team all took sushi lessons together and now they're gonna make it as a fundraiser."

Caitlin watched one guy try to roll raw tuna onto sticky rice. Another guy dropped something slippery and picked it up again. He looked around quickly and tossed it into a pot.

"Do you want water polo sushi," Bret asked.

"Wow," said Caitlin slowly. "That looks like a great recipe for everyone to get really sick."

"Yeah," said Bret. "We'll find something else."

A girl with pigtails tried to warn them about global warming.

o o o

The freshman girl's body was warm as she lay next to Bret on his bed. Her white shirt hung crumpled on the chair next to her pants. Easier than he ever could have dreamed.

They both did a shot from the bad gin, number six for Bret, and she ran her hand along his chest as the distant music pounded. Her fingers caught on his necklace. Bret stared at the stolen road signs on the wall. YIELD. VOTE FOR PROP 297. ASSISTANCE 15 MI.

"What's this," asked the girl, holding the medallion up.

"It's my necklace," mumbled Bret. "Do you understand it?"

"Oh wow," the girl burbled, peering closely. "That looks really cool."

It was really cool, and it came from a proud continent that had sunk under the aquamarine waves of the Western Sea at a time when the skies were all wrong, more than seven millennia before Mr. and Mrs. H. Winslow Stanton had met at the Princeton formal and begun a relationship that would eventually lead to the production of Bret.

The Mediterranean vacation, suddenly trendy again, had beckoned Winslow to the rocky shores of Crete, and Bret found himself—a couple of summers before college— dragged along to legitimize the already quite consummated relationship between his dad and his new stepmom. Mrs. H. Winslow had bailed out a couple of years earlier with lots of cash.

His dad fucked the bitch in their rustic hotel room as a sea breeze billowed out the thin white curtain and bright purple flowers pressed in the open window, and Bret wandered a whitewashed city that stood against the deep sapphire bay of Souda like a Parliament Lights ad.

He stopped in a steep and winding street at a little shop doorway crowded with driftwood racks of chains and pendants. Maybe they had a hemp necklace like his sailing buddies from Nantucket wore. He looked around, listening to the sea roar behind his back, standing in a cool breeze that the dark interior exhaled onto the blazing white road. He only noticed the old woman waiting inside when he turned to leave. Dressed in pure black, a darkness in darkness.

Her eyes stared into his. A wrinkled leather face, tanned by subtropical sun and weathered by salty air. "Okay," she said. "You are the right one."

She turned back into the shop. "Wait here," she called as her cloak receded into the darkness.

Bret stood around for a little while. He felt like the peasants were staring at him as they passed. He felt dumb. He leaned up against the wall. Little bits of warm plaster broke off and dusted his shirt and neck.

Then the old woman came back. She had something in her hand: a chain with a small golden disc, about one inch across. "You will buy this," she announced.

"Why," asked Bret. "What is it?"

"It is a last piece of the most ancient of civilizations, although its origins are a dream and it predates that thrice-circular empire by countless eternities. I will charge you one thousand drachmas."

"Huh," mumbled Bret. He took a closer look because he felt she wanted him to. "Is that real gold?"

"What is gold?" cried the woman. "It is orichalcum, the Platonic metal."

"One thousand drachmas is like four bucks, right," asked Bret.

"It is less," said the woman.

Bret waffled. The woman's eyes bulged out. She began to shriek and wave the disc around by its chain. It flashed in the sun. "From this fragment you may reconstruct the whole! The amulet of the Pleroma is the key to life and death, pain and pleasure, joy and sorrow, fear and desire—"

Bret looked around hurriedly. All the peasants were gawking at him and babbling in their staccato tongue. "Fine," he said. He pulled out a bill. "Do you have change?"

Now, the front of this necklace had a picture of a rising sun. The back had a picture of a setting sun. The suns were ringed by tiny detailed glyphs: of kings, of priests, of distant moons, of warriors and machines. Intricate geometric writing circled the figures. Bret put it on because he thought it looked cool, and not all that seventies.

The night after, he was wearing it in a bar in Megala

Chorafia when he met a girl from England and got laid for the first time ever. He thought maybe that was its special magic—luck, luck with women?—but after that first night he always seemed to be on a roller-coaster ride that climbed sharp new heights just to plunge into long new drops. Every day opened bright and chaotic, so much to do, so much going on, no time to sit and think about meanings. So he just had no idea.

7

"No idea," said the freshman girl. She let go of the necklace and fixed her hair.

"I'm taking off," said Bret, pulling on his shirt. "You can stay here if you want."

The girl's mouth opened a little and she looked down at her hands. Bret got his pants and shoes on. She didn't seem to be going anywhere, just looking at her hands, so he shut the door behind himself and walked right into another girl. This one had weird teeth.

"Oh!" said the girl with weird teeth.

She was holding a yellow cup and waiting outside his room. "What were you doing in the women's bathroom?" she demanded. "You've been in there forever."

"Huh," asked Bret and then he saw the sign on his door and shrugged.

The beat downstairs was so loud, the upstairs walls were shaking a little. Bret walked along the hall. He really didn't want to see any more of that freshman girl. Or the weird-teeth girl outside his room, even though he'd just met her. He'd go away for a while and give them some time to clear out.

Crowds filled the corridor, kinda familiar faces spilling up around the bend in the big staircase. Bret stood for a second, watching them emerge into the pale green light of the landing from a downstairs darkness where colored strobes flashed.

"Heyyyy! Bret!" some short guy said, and Bret did the snap with him. The guy's hand was cold and slimy and Bret panicked. He had to get moving. He pressed against the far wall, put out an elbow, slipped clear.

At the other end of the hall a long line from the real second-floor bathroom curled around the corner. Bret squeezed past the column of bodies.

A platinum blond girl with a blue cup was saying, "—and I was like, 'That's Dolce, my ass!'"

Her friend rolled her eyes, ran her fingernails along the wall. "What'd he say?"

Bret pushed by some guy trying to be punk in a mesh cap.

Three girls opened the stairway door. "Oh my God, is that the line," one of them asked. She had a yellow cup.

"Yeah," said Bret, descending.

"Is there a bathroom on the third floor?" she called after Bret's back.

"Yeah," said Bret.

In the stairwell he had to squeeze around a really drunk guy with a green cup who had dropped a handful of change down the steps.

A shower of silver coins cascaded into a tray as bells rang and lights flashed. An old man seated at the machine eagerly swept his hoard into his flimsy plastic bucket and looked up.

The old man wasn't getting his drink, because the cocktail waitress had stopped pushing her trolley. She was talking to Masters with her head cocked and her hand on her hip. Bret stood watching on an endless dark blue casino carpet with ornate golden leaves that stretched under rows and rows of flashing slot machines.

Then Masters was there, grinning, holding up a slip of white paper. "Yeah, I got her number," he said.

"You are too fucking good," said Bret, and they did the snap.

Masters pressed the slip of paper into Bret's hand. "Don't say your Big Bro doesn't hook you up," he said. "I get these no problem."

Bret looked at the paper. DAWN plus phone number scribbled in blue ink. "Dude, you're giving this to me," he asked.

Masters smiled and clapped Bret on the shoulder. "Hey, you picked me. She said she's also a stripper at Déjà Vu and she does it for fun."

Masters pushed open a mirrored door and Bret followed him out into the warm dark night.

"Sweet!" Bret said, folding up the paper and sticking it in his pocket. "Thanks! I guess I'll get a fifteen-buck room and give her a call."

He turned around and craned up to figure out what hotel he had been in, but all he could see from the awkward angle was the corner of a massive light sign that cycled through color changes. Lower down, a wall of palm trees bathed in pink neon.

"Maybe you could bring her by the Winnie later on and she could do like a show," said Masters as they walked across a parking lot. A bunch of actives and pledges had driven out past desert windmills in a few campers, parked somewhere.

Bret laughed. "Yeah, after me she's gonna be too tired to do a show," he said.

The strip was ablaze, flashing bulbs around them. Off to the sides rose towering buildings drenched in colored light. Cars poured past, a wide avenue of motion.

Masters looked around. "To the Luxor!" he cried. He looked at his watch. "Oh, shit, we were supposed to like be there already."

"I'm sure half my class is still wandering around," said Bret.

Masters rubbed his cheek. "Dude, your pledge class cracks me up," he said. "Who's that guy Hollingsworth is trying to make like the perfect DD?"

"Oh, yeah, Dave," said Bret.

"What's he doing," asked Masters. "He has to like go to church?"

"Yeah," said Bret. "He has to go to chapel every week and read the Book of Mormon cover-to-cover. Hollingsworth wants him to convert because Mormons can't drink, and then we'd always have a designated driver."

"Hollingsworth's a sick fuck," laughed Masters. "I don't make you do that shit."

Across the street to the left, hundreds of people crowded around the arched marble courtyard of a Renaissance palace awash with light, where figures in colorful costume whirled and pirouetted.

"Thanks," said Bret.

"Yeah, I just tell you to be a good PAK. Dude, the fucking accomplishment is getting the bid."

"Yeah," asked Bret.

"Yeah, no doubt," said Masters. "A lot of people are going to be jealous of you 'cause you get a life and they don't. You just gotta remember PAK hooks you up, and be like grateful. You can't do any better at Pony."

"Oh, yeah," said Bret.

To the right, hundreds of people crowded on boardwalks

around a miniature ocean where a pirate ship rocked under cannon blasts.

Masters looked into the neon night. "If there weren't any PAK, you'd just be a random living a shit-ass boring little life, and then it'd be time to graduate, and that'd be it. So you gotta love it, Bret. Love all one hundred and forty-three chapters, including the first one founded at?"

"Miami University of Ohio in 1857," said Bret.

"See, you know your shit," said Masters.

"We got a test next week," said Bret.

Then they were at the Luxor. This one brilliant beam erupted from the top of the black glass pyramid. It punched upward through the ionosphere like a light saber into satellite space, connecting earth to heaven. But of course it was only light soaring into air.

The Ping-Pong ball flew into space from Bret's open hand. It hit the inside of a cup, spun around in a rattling orbit and landed with a plop in pale beer.

Sheffield's girlfriend shrieked. "Oh, who're the losers!" She nodded and pointed at Eddie Kirkley and Taylor McLaughlen, and high-fived Bret and hugged him.

This game was really easy. You just had to curve the ball right.

"Nice one!" somebody yelled.

The small room off the side hall was packed, dim, hot

and sticky. It resonated a throbbing beat. Maybe a hundred bodies, mostly guys. A lot of green cups, a few yellow—why be near the beer if you're never getting any?

Exhibition beer pong was going down on a board laid across the foosball table.

"Eric!" screamed Sheffield's girlfriend. "We kicked ass!"

Sheffield was standing with Craig at the front of the crowd around the table, bouncing to the music.

"You're not paying attention to me!" said his girlfriend, pulling on his shirt. She swiveled and started talking to Bret instead.

"Hey, stud," she said to him.

"Hey, hottie," he said to her.

She laughed. "I don't deserve to talk to you," she said. "You're gonna be like Fraternity Man of the Year."

"Huh," asked Bret.

She cupped her hands around his ear. "You're probably gonna be Fraternity Man of the Year," she screamed.

"Dude, you missed like all the shots," Eddie was saying to Taylor. "You definitely have to drink like two-thirds of it."

Bret had twisted away and his ear was in shock from her shouting. "What," he asked. Sheffield's girlfriend cupped her hands again and Bret backed off. "No, I *heard* you, but what?"

"Didn't you get a message or something," she asked. The air was very hot and humid, a sour smell of spilled drinks.

"No," said Bret.

Sheffield's girlfriend tossed her hair back. "We were talking about Greek Recognition Awards at ISC and we had the final round of names. It's you and like two other people."

She glanced over at Sheffield. "The other guys aren't that cool, though, so I wouldn't like worry about it."

"Holy shit," said Bret.

"You'll know on Monday. Just like remember us little people," she said.

Bret looked up at a metal fire sprinkler in a red wire cage above his head.

He had had a chapter leadership position. He was fine gradewise. He had said okay to being on the mandatory Alcohol Awareness panel. He played a sport. He did philanthropy. A bunch of students knew him. He had cosigned a letter last quarter to the *Pony Express* about unfair stereotyping of Greeks.

"Hey, who's up next game?" somebody was yelling.

All the stuff he was and did, they must have been the right things. They added up to Fraternity Man of the Year. He blinked.

"Taylor's being a pussy and he won't finish the beers," Eddie complained.

"Dude, fuck you, I'm drinking them," said Taylor.

"Fuck, I'll finish them," said Bret.

"Taylor has to finish them," said Eddie.

"Dude, I'm twenty-one," said Bret. "I gotta do the twenty-one."

"You're twenty-*one*?" said Sheffield's girlfriend, staring.

"Yeah," said Bret. "How old did you think I was?"

She shrugged. "I don't know. Not twenty-one."

"Older," asked Bret. "Younger?"

"Either," she said.

Bret picked two half-cups off the table and poured them together into one. The music ratcheted up to thundering.

It hit Bret as he was drinking and the cup vibrated in his hand. He finished the beer but no one saw. Sheffield's girlfriend was kinda swaying. Other guys were eyeing the table. Eddie moshed into Taylor and now they were trying to knock each other over.

"I'm taking a piss," said Bret, but no one heard him because it was so loud. He plunged forward into sweat and bodies.

A group of giggling girls with heavy makeup clustered by the wall and Bret caught the metallic flash of braces. Holy shit, so young, must be East Emerson High School kids who had snuck in tonight.

Except for one big problem, Bret loved Poniente when he came to visit during spring term of his senior year in high school. He never saw his room host, randomly assigned Chad Davys from Santa Cruz. Bret spent a couple of hours in the empty room, just staring at the guy's surfboard and mountain bike, and then he decided to check out the party scene.

Some drunk sophomore in the hall told him that PAK was bumping. He decided to roll by. The sophomore could barely stand up, so Bret went to a resident assistant—an RA—for directions. The RA had covered the lights in her room with tie-dye wraps. She was reading a sociology text-book on her futon and everything smelled like cinnamon.

Her little flower nose ring wrinkled up when he men-tioned PAK. "They're assholes." She pursed her lips. When he left she warned him to "be careful," but she said it flat and jaded as if she knew he wouldn't listen to her.

In fact he didn't care what she thought; she looked like a friendless crunchy granola chick. A classic RA case, he later learned. But between swigs from her Nalgene bottle, she had told him the way to his future home.

The theme was "Pimps 'n' Hos." Bret scored a hat with a feather in it from someone passed out outside, so he was representing minimalist styles. A couple of the guys he was chilling with in the barroom, A-Rod and Stevens, thought he was a frosh and it was fucking incredible when they found out he was still in high school.

He ended up doing a couple of lines in Stevens's room and then banging some 22-year-old girl against the wall. He got major props and moved in with Stevens for the next few days, after taping a note to that effect on Chad's snowboard.

In the mornings he woke up to a warm dry breeze and the sound of construction from the window.

The night before he flew back to Massachusetts, then-President Miller Haviland told him, "Uh, Bret, you should definitely come by during Rush."

The one bad thing happened five hours before his flight, when he was in Krasner Auditorium for a presentation about the academic opportunities offered at Poniente. (Some associate dean was saying, "You may have heard that college is not the real world. . . .") Bret was bored and was looking through the folder of materials they had all been given.

He glanced down at a page and his stomach dropped. It talked about the Punto Nitido National Observatory, a 210-foot radio telescope perched on a hill at the edge of campus. The observatory was headed by Nobel Prize-winning astrophysicist Anthony Abbamonte.

The world spun around and Bret sat holding his head. He almost decided not to come to Poniente but then he changed his mind. Despite the fact he felt so sick that he wanted to throw up right then and there in the auditorium.

8

Bret felt a little queasy and almost thought he might puke in the bathroom toilet—but no way, it was way too early. He stared at himself in the mirror for an undefined amount of time while someone pounded on the door. Eventually the person stopped knocking, and Bret opened the door and walked into a guy wearing a UCONN cap. They impacted pretty hard, making the guy spill his beer.

"What the fuck," cried Bret, shaking off his hand. Beer had splashed onto the part of his shirt with the Pacific Outfitters shield, and as far as Bret was concerned it had better not stain.

"I'm really sorry, man," said the guy, who had a yellow cup. Pretty low in the rankings.

"Yeah, whatever," said Bret, turning away. "Cocksucker."

The guy looked him over closely as the crowd kept

r name isn't Bret Stanton, is it?" he called

ds of a caravan of two girls, hands linked,

r way to the bathroom door.

ed around. "Yeah," he said. "Who are you?"

's mouth dropped open and he started laughing. "Shit! That's totally unreal. I don't believe it. Un-fucking-real."

Bret asked again: "Who are you?"

"Darron Moore? I went to school with you for like ten years."

"Darron?" Bret wanted to give him the snap but couldn't because people kept pouring past. The music was really loud.

"We all wondered what happened to you after eighth grade when you didn't go to Madison—"

Some huge Southerner Bret had met through one of his rugby friends stopped in the flow of traffic between him and Darron. "You partying, man?" the rugby player drawled, totally trashed.

Bret smiled and nodded and slapped him on the back. He wouldn't budge.

"Yeah, we moved to Dayfield," Bret called around him.

"You never came back to visit us or anything," said Darron.

The Southerner fixed Bret with an empty gaze. "Wait, did you say you're partying," he asked slowly, turning his green cup.

"Yeah, I'm partying," mumbled Bret. He looked around the rugby guy at Darron, who was trapped behind an almost identical group of girls in white blouses and black capri pants, not moving farther away but caught, inaccessible. "Hey, bro, I didn't really have much time free, you know."

"You had vacations, didn't you?" Darron shouted over the bass line.

"Are you partyin' or are you fucking *partying*!?" demanded the big guy. Traffic had diverted around him.

Bret didn't know how to answer anyone. The capri pants girls burst out laughing. They all had blue cups, except a fatter one who had green.

Darron started to laugh again as he peered through the ring of girls. "Hey, remember when we were in Mrs. Janowitz's class and she would always look at the ceiling when she was teaching, and we got everyone to move their chairs in closer, slowly, so when she looked down at the end of class she couldn't move anywhere because we were there and she freaked out and started screaming and shit?"

The rugby player started fighting with his girlfriend.

Bret stared at Darron. An image out of focus, the contrast all wrong, the audio track entirely different. Celluloid from some old decaying movie crudely grafted in, the patches so rough that weakened seams might tear.

"No," Bret said eventually. "Do you even go to school here?"

Darron's mouth dropped slightly open. Bret looked back

wordlessly and then the crowd shifted and Bret moved with it. Bodies fed him past an alcove where the pay phone was ringing unanswered.

The house alarm bell was ringing as a brick sailed past Bret through a window shattering in a storm of glass. He spun away and covered his head, but one sliver tore a little cut in the side of his arm.

"Fuck!" screamed Carl Corday. He ran past to shore up the front door with a baseball bat.

The house intercom speaker in the middle of the side hall clicked on, breathless: "Three guys coming for the chapter room window." The intercom never said anything good.

The side of Bret's arm stung and some blood was dripping out. Pressed under the window frame, he grabbed the brick. He took a quick look out to the lawn where Fijis massed in darkness with pipes and chains and hammers and BBQ lighters, hurled the brick, and dropped down again.

(The PAKs and the Fijis had always really hated each other, and now some girl Jessica who was the ex-girlfriend of one of the Fiji seniors had been at a PAK party and the Fijis said some PAK, unclear who, put this drug in her drink and raped her.)

A quick yell among other screams from outside.

The intercom, hysterical: "We've got guys in the kitchen door!"

Suddenly a leg appeared in the smashed window frame.

"Entering!" screamed Bret.

(The drug was called GHB and had no color and no smell. It could stop breathing and send someone into a coma, especially someone who had been drinking.)

Bret jumped up and grabbed the guy's leg and twisted it and tried to shove him back out as the guy struggled and tried to kick him in the face with a black DC shoe.

"Fucking PAK shitbag," the guy was ranting as his foot thrashed.

(The PAKs said fuck, they weren't rapists, and the girl could do what she wanted and her ex-boyfriend was a jealous motherfucker because Fijis weren't enough for her and she wanted the PAK dilz. The girl was unavailable for comment.)

Shattering glass and yells from outside, a dull crunch somewhere inside. A group of five more Fijis raced up in the darkness beyond the open window.

"Entering!" Bret screamed as loud as he could. The guy's foot connected and turned the world to exploding light and pain.

(So the Fijis had attacked, and later on this night the PAKs would rally and take vengeance on the Fiji house.)

Brief impressions: Tom Hunter looking around the corner from the common room, screaming, "Dude, I got them," charging down the hall with a metal bar from the kitchen shelves.

Although his face throbbed and he felt dizzy, Bret felt safe, secure. It was clear who you were and who you were fighting. He felt like he was part of a team.

(The police would come late, everyone dispersed and no one talking. In fact, a lot, a lot of people wanted to keep things quiet because it hardly looked good when trying to bring management consulting and product design and market research and accountancy/auditing and public relations and financial brokerage firms to interview at Poniente.)

"Yo, pledge, are you okay," Tom Hunter asked Bret when the area was clear.

Bret had blood all over his face and on his hands and everywhere. "Yeah," he said.

"Come on," said Hunter, pulling him up. "We need you in the kitchen."

He tore a fire extinguisher off the wall and thrust it into Bret's arms. "Hit 'em in the face," he panted as they raced down the hall over shattered glass and flipped couches.

(In the end no one really cared about the girl or whatever. But damn if it wasn't a good excuse to fight.)

Distant screams and crashes. "Three climbing toward the balcony," announced the intercom speakers.

The DJ's huge speakers matted the colored light beams that strobed through the air, swallowing them up completely. The lights glistened on the sapphire jacket of one of the security guards. He was leaning against the wall next to the phone, which rang softly under the music. Bret jostled its hook and the noise stopped. Years of scribbled phone numbers and messages dripped from flaking plaster. The guard looked built and mean.

Bret tapped him on the shoulder. He turned, his jacket rustling. "Yes," the guard asked with a slight Mexican accent.

"Yeah, hi," said Bret. "I live here. There's a guy in the house who's wearing a hat that says UCONN on it. Like *U-C-O-N-N*. He's been causing some problems."

"Really," said the guard, raising his eyebrows. "Do you know where he is?"

Bret gestured outward. "In the crowd somewhere. Maybe he should be, um . . ."

The guard held his walkie-talkie to his mouth. It crackled with static. "We will remove him."

Bret patted the guard absently on the shoulder. "Thank you," he said, wandering away. He was supposed to have another drink.

In the barroom, Rob was directing the pledges to haul a bucket into the middle of the floor. "Keg stands!" he laughed, pounding Bret on the shoulder. "You're doing a keg stand, you fucking drinking *machine*!"

A row of fake machines. Bret sat on the close-cropped tan carpet and stared at the plastic robots lined up before him.

He pointed at the leftmost robot, which was cooler

than the others. "I like that one better," he announced.

Wendy and his mom exchanged glances. "He likes the Rastel one better," moaned Wendy.

His mom gave him a big smile of victory from her low-slung leather chair. She got up and kneeled down next to Bret and readjusted her suit. She put a hand on his shoulder. He looked at her big gold bracelet.

"Honey," she said brightly. "Could you tell Mommy why you like that one better than the blue one?"

Bret cocked his head and thought a little. "It turns into a plane and, see, it can shoot lasers from its eyes, and the blue one can just be a tank and it doesn't make any noise."

His mom nodded sagely and turned to Wendy. "Uh-huh. It's the sound thing. We've been over this with them forever. Across the board, kids in his demo like the sound."

Wendy leaned down toward Bret. "Would you like the blue one better if it made the laser sound?"

"Maybe. I guess so."

Wendy sighed and turned to his mom. "I think it's pretty clear. No jinxes, but I'd like to say we've got Gemco for the long haul."

"You agree with most other kids about the sound, Bret," his mom said. "And that's great."

"It is," asked Bret.

"You bet," said his mom.

Wendy laughed. "Principle number one: The majority is right. A marketing genius in the making."

"Bret's my little focus group," his mom said as she packed up her briefcase.

The latch clicked shut and she turned around. She kissed her fingers and laid them lightly on his forehead. "I'll be working late tonight, honey," she said, standing up. "I've got to go tell some people about your important ideas."

"I love you, Mommy," said Bret.

Some piece of art with lines and grids took up half the office wall. Beneath it, printed in block lettering, IT HAS ITS HIGH POINTS AND ITS LOW POINTS. IT ALL DEPENDS ON YOUR VANTAGE POINT.

On the way out, right before the door closed, she turned and promised Bret, "I'll have Martina get you some ice cream on the way home."

And then she left. Wendy didn't say anything as she passed behind Bret on her way out.

A girl stumbled past behind Bret, bumped into him and spilled beer down his back from her blue cup. She tried to apologize and collapsed in uncontrollable laughter.

"Keg stand!" someone was hollering. "Birthday boy does a keg stand!"

Brothers and others crowded around him. Bodies pressed him and he grabbed on to the dented metal edge. He let himself be lifted upside down. . . .

"Yeah, Bret!" someone bellowed by his ear. He took the thick rubber tube in his mouth.

People chanted: "Bret! Bret! Bret!" The music pounded on all around him. *"California knows how to party!"* It felt like some state law required this song to be played at least every weekend.

Ryan Yeager(meister) pressed the valve and the liquid began to flow, slightly bitter. Natty Lite open-party keg shit because even though this was invite only it seemed like everyone and their moms had one. You didn't want randoms drinking your expensive stuff—everyone got the same beer regardless of cup color. Liquid poured the wrong way, upward, defying gravity, pulled into his body by the action of throat muscles.

"One . . . ," a cry rose up, "two . . . three . . ." Nate crouched down and gave an impassioned performance of counting out the seconds on his fingers and gave up in confusion when he got to ten.

The flow, its enumeration—this seemed like a beautiful system, a peaceful system that promised some sort of release, some assurance that *what he was doing was right,* and rage and disappointment exploded in Bret's mind as he choked on the liquid and his lungs began to explode at only nineteen.

They quickly set him down and Bret staggered backward, dizzy with the world's spinning around some point that was most definitely not him. Some fat guy's face loomed up large: "Are you okay, buddy?" Bret nodded and the coughing quickly died. There was a collective breath taken and then . . .

"Yeah, Bret!" probably the same person as before bellowed.

His brothers shook, embraced, high-fived, *props*-ed him. He was *the man*. He *fuckin' kicked ass*. He was twenty-one and this was legal!

And then the people faded back into the crowd and Bret wandered around a little in confusion. The music thundered, the colored lights swiveled. He slid along the glass-windowed doors, pressed by the masses of dancing bodies, writhing rhythmically more or less, searching for an opening to escape to the cooler air of the backyard. His face looked back at him from glass.

Bret leaned his head against the mirror and made eye contact. Where am I? he wondered in momentary panic.

Reflected behind him, the cameraman crouched at the back of the bathroom. His red light glowed, recording. Bret could relax a bit—none of his life would be lost, everything was captured on film.

The cameraman pivoted as the bathroom door swung open. It was Wes. "Dude, Bret, parasailing time! Get off your ass. We're renting the ATVs!"

"Yeah, hang on a sec," said Bret, and shut the door with his foot. The cameraman swiveled back. Did he want tension building? Bret could hear the rock 'n' rap soundtrack kicking in, intercut with sound bites of him and Wes bashing each other.

He put his forehead back on the mirror. Just him and the cameraman now. No escape from the lens, that penetration of total vision.

"I'm usually cooler," *he mumbled. Pounding headache; bright sunlight from the window reflected through the mirror into his eyes.*

The man glared cycloptically, somewhere behind his machine. "C'mon, buddy, no talking to me. I'm not here."

Right.

In the mirror Bret pulled a white Volcom cap on diagonally as Wes called behind the door: "Dude, Craig was so fucked up last night he put his head through the drywall!"

"Hells yeah!" *Bret yelled back.* "C-sketch is out of control!"

But a brief look passed across his face that said I'm acting, *kind of a slackness of facial expression. Eyes defocused, somewhere far away.*

The red light glowed reproachfully. It couldn't handle this level of character development.

"C'mon, buddy, don't do that," *said the cameraman.*

"Sorry," *pleaded Bret. Outside, rising turquoise surf; more distant, people yelling and pounding music. The cameraman turned to the window for a second to get some footage of a huge inflatable Corona bottle amid waving palms.*

"Damn, the sky's blue," *Wes was yelling.* "Para-fucking-sailing!"

Bret thought the cameraman was distracted, and he said, very softly, "The sky's blue because of . . ."

The air felt warm. It had a salty urgency. "Of refraction."

Oh, shit. The mirror showed the glowing red light trained on the back of his head. Daggers of sight stripped all barriers away.

He tried to pretend he was just singing an old club song: "I have a blue house with a blue window; blue is the color of all that I wear. . . ."

The cameraman got so pissed he almost put the machine down. Bret closed his eyes and rubbed his aching forehead. He was trapped in a nightmare reflection of lenses. "My bad."

"What are you doing?" the cameraman demanded.

"I'm sorry," Bret repeated desperately. "I really am. I thought you weren't listening to me."

"The mic gets everything. The kids who watch Spring Break Undercover don't want to see that shit. So chill out with it, okay?"

"Are you a woman? What are you doing in there?" Craig screamed. Bret thought he heard him and Wes playing some quick quarters for amaretto shots in the other room.

Bret put on his necklace in silence. The cameraman didn't say anything.

Poor guy. He deserved a better subject. Bret vowed to make it up to him and redeem himself for the viewing audience.

Tonight at the foam party, he was going to take all his clothes off and freak that hot Texan girl he'd met at the Jacuzzi thing. Either that or get into a parasailing accident—he hadn't figured out which yet. Maybe both.

He sprayed on some Polo Sport. They'd have to blur over the bottle's logo. But he doubted that shoddy segment would ever make it through the editing room. He opened the door.

9

Bret shut the door behind him. The house wrapped its solid three-story C shape around the backyard. Ripples of colored light passed through the wall of glass doors and washed over an ocean of faces. Tall palm trees rustled against a sky of marbleized ebony electrified with a spray of stars and nebulae.

Cooler out here, with a faint breeze and a sharp smell of cigarette smoke mixed with sweeter scents. People hung around in small groups talking, holding cups, laughing. Bret passed through the faces. Fresh sensation, sweat evaporating from his hair and forehead. He nodded to a few people, shot them the point.

Tiny shadows flitted by above, bats flying night missions. Bret could kinda guess where the sound waves were by watching the bats move.

In the middle of the yard, Kevin Whalen was sitting on a picnic table with his feet on the bench and some girl sitting between his legs. Scattered around the tabletop: a bunch of partly full cups and some empty ones with ashes and butts at the bottom.

"We got the hot tub fired up," Kevin said.

"Yeah," asked Bret.

"Yeah," said Kevin. "Go check it out."

"Definitely recommended," said the girl. Her long hair wet, a towel wrapped around her waist.

"Tight," said Bret. "I'm going."

He threaded through the groups to the back of the yard, where clouds of steam rose and passed into air. The hot tub pressed up against the rust-colored wooden slats of the perimeter fence.

A couple of senior guys—Dwight Graden, sitting on the edge, and Ken Wannamaker—and three girls Bret didn't know. Oh, wait, he knew one of them. Kiki or something.

"Lookin' pretty steamy over here," Bret said.

Dwight had a big box of Franzia wine and was squeezing the top and pouring it into his mouth.

"It's *really* steamy," said one of the girls, laughing.

"Jump in, bro," said Ken, just a head floating on the water.

"Oh, what the hell," said Bret. He stripped down to his boxers and hung his clothes on the fence. The girls were laughing. "Yeah!" one of them said.

Bret's necklace glinted but no one noticed it. He splashed into the tub. "Ohhhh," he said, sinking into hot water.

"I'm drinking to that," said Dwight, trying to angle the box right so wine would come out.

Kiki looked over at the shield on his shirt. "I see you're rocking the Pacific Outfitters," she said.

"Oh, yeah," said Bret.

"I left like a month after you did," said Kiki. She was wearing a lot of pink lip gloss and she had a really good tan.

Dwight put the Franzia box on Ken's head.

"Yeah, they changed the schedule, right," asked Bret.

"Oh, what the fuck," said Ken, reaching up and taking the box.

"Well, I kinda got fired," said Kiki. "I had bad PPT."

"Oh," said Bret.

"What's PPT," asked one of the other girls.

"Pants per transaction," Kiki was saying. "It's like . . . God, what's it like?"

"It's like how many pants you sell," Bret explained. "They want you to sell a lot of pants because people keep coming back to the same place to get pants."

"Hi, I'm Brianna," said the girl who had asked. Her eyelashes were really long.

"What's up. Bret." They shook hands. Steam curled up around them.

The tops of some heads were passing by the other side

of the pickets. Bret heard a voice saying, "—guy was a total asshole."

"So I get it," Brianna said. "So it's like whether you're selling a lot of pants."

"Yeah, basically," said Kiki. She turned to Bret. "But I got an eight."

"Nice," said Bret.

Dwight was looking around at the crowds. A couple of pledges walked by the hot tub, laughing and pushing each other.

Ken's crew-cut head yelled at them: "Watch out for the fucking Source!"

The pledges jumped, looking around nervously. Then they got quiet and hurried away.

"What's that," asked the other girl.

"Long story," said Dwight, and he and Bret laughed.

A big silence. Then Dwight pulled the box out of the steaming water. It was soaking wet, a total mess. "Fuck this," he said, and ripped the box apart, tossing sodden strips of cardboard over the edge, pulling the shiny silver foil bag of wine from inside. He tore off the spout.

"Here's to Pony rugby," he said, holding up the bag.

"Dude, give me some of that," Bret said to Dwight. "I gotta do the twenty-one."

"Stanton, you're legal today?" said Dwight, passing the bag when he was done. "Watch out for this man!"

"Better believe," said Bret, laughing.

He bunched up the torn end of the silver bag and tilted his head back and began to swallow what he figured was a unit. The wine tasted kinda like battery acid. He realized he was staring up beyond the silver bag at a bright spray of stars, and that in fact he couldn't actually see anything besides the bag and the stars. Somewhere distant and lateral rushed the beat from the house and talking and laughter.

When he finished the wine he was surprised, because there hadn't been much in the bag and now it was totally empty. But he stayed like that a few more seconds, facing up, pretending to swallow. He breathed in deeply through his nose, a few calm breaths of empty air. Then he snapped his head down and beamed. When he ripped the silver bag open, only a couple of drops fell out. Red hit the steaming water, shimmered, spread out, dissolved into clarity.

"You killed it!" said Dwight as Bret chucked the remains of the bag and torn silver fluttered to dark wet grass.

"Yay!" said Kiki, and she started clapping. Brianna clapped too.

Ken's eyes had drifted shut. Dwight peered down at him. "Look at this fucker," he said.

"I'm cold," said the third girl, getting out of the hot tub. Steam rose off her wet skin.

"Are you okay," asked Kiki.

"Yeah," said the girl. "I think I'm going back in." She

got her towel from the fence and wrapped herself in it. She pattered off into the crowd, leaving a trail of shrinking footprints on the concrete.

"Has anyone got any E," Brianna asked after a while.

"Fuck that shit," said Bret.

Brianna held up her hands and glanced at the water, smiling. "Sorry."

"Whoa," said Kiki, making a time-out sign. "Backtrack. When did *you* become all like 'Just Say No'?"

"No, Ecstasy just sucks," said Bret.

Dwight splashed him. "What are you *talking* about, Stanton?" He laughed.

They all sat there in silence in clouds of steam watching Ken's head slide down the side of the hot tub into the water. Pulsing beat, reflected ripples.

Bret had draped his hand over the side of the tub. Brianna saw the scar on the back. "What's that from," she asked. He shrugged.

The water was very hot and heavy and he felt a little dizzy, dead-ended in bubbles rising and swirling. His leg brushed against Kiki's.

"Oh, shit," he said. "I gotta do my other units." He stood up with a splash of water and shower of drops. Everyone looked at him. Cold air.

He climbed out of the hot tub, swung his feet onto the ground. "Whose towel is this?" A blue one on the fence.

Blank looks. "Not mine," offered Dwight.

"Tight," said Bret, and dried off with it.

"Your boxers are soaked!" said Brianna.

"I'm going commando," said Bret, and took them off under the towel and pulled on his jeans and shirt and socks and shoes. He hung the boxers on the fence.

"Later," he said through steam.

Steam curled out of Caitlin's cup of coffee. Bret had a burger and fries while she poked around a chicken Caesar salad.

They sat at a white plastic table under the shade of low palm trees. Conversations, guys and girls talking and laughing at dozens of tables around them.

"Any, uh, relationships," Caitlin asked. "Girlfriend, anything like that?"

A decent breeze blew her hair and rattled the paper signs taped onto the third-floor terrace of the building behind them. LOW FARES TO MAZATLAN! ΣX DERBY DAYS! JUNIOR FORMAL.

Bret squirted more ketchup on his fries. "I was going out with this girl a couple months ago," he said.

"How did that go," asked Caitlin.

"I don't know," said Bret. "Whatever. How about you?"

"No," Caitlin said, and smiled. "I'm too busy being overwhelmed by college."

"Huh," asked Bret.

"There's like so many choices, you know?" said Caitlin. "Like I started out thinking I wanted to do anthropology, but

now I'm kinda leaning toward art history." She pushed back her hair. "I didn't even know what 'a capella' was three months ago, and now I'm trying out for next year."

"What is 'a capella,'" asked Bret.

"It's those singing groups," said Caitlin. "You guys don't have them?"

"I don't know," said Bret. "Maybe." He chewed his burger. "I guess I thought about doing pre-med like Masters, but there's too many early classes."

Warm wind. A fly buzzed around their table and landed on the napkin dispenser.

"So business is what you really want to do," she asked. "Kinda like your dad?"

"Sure," said Bret.

"Huh," said Caitlin. "I didn't really think of you as the business type."

"That's weird," said Bret, rolling his straw wrapper into a ball. "Why wouldn't I be the business type?"

A silence as Caitlin pushed some lettuce around her plate. When she looked up he was still watching her. "I mean," she said, "it's fine if you are."

She glanced down. The fly flitted away.

"So what kind of stuff do you want to see here," Bret asked. "I can show you like the beach and the house and stuff, I guess."

A crowd of about twenty people shuffled into view around the building. A few blue East Emerson High shirts, *a lot of parents' gray hair and glasses. A guy with a Hurley cap walked backward at the front of the group. Owing to the bunch of steps near the cliffs, Pony tour guides who walked backward had to have a lot of faith in themselves. If your tour was unimpressed, they wouldn't warn you as the steps drew near. Bret's tour guide kept demanding that everyone tell her they were "good-good!" in unison. They let the freak fall.*

"Okay!" said Hurley-cap guy. "This is the Copeland Family Student Union here on your left." He pointed at the big tan building. "The Union was built in 1964 and is commonly known as the U. The U is a popular place for students to grab lunch and also contains Poniente's bookstore, credit union, and Office of Student Life. We—"

He saw Bret sitting at the table and interrupted himself briefly to say, "Hello, Doctor Stanton."

Bret raised a hand in greeting and gave a curt professorial nod.

The girls whispered and the parents muttered while they tried to figure out if he was really a professor. The crowd worked its way onward. ("Even if you never set foot in a classroom, you will go to the U. . . .")

Caitlin started laughing. "That's so funny!" she said. "Who is that guy?"

"Some guy who lives down my hall in Towers," said Bret.

Caitlin picked out a really big crouton. "Do you guys hang out," she asked.

"Not really," said Bret. "He's not pledging anywhere or anything."

"You could still hang out," said Caitlin.

Bret shrugged. "Masters says you've always got to wonder what's wrong with the GDIs. Either they couldn't get bids or for some weird reason they didn't want to pledge."

"What are GDIs," asked Caitlin.

"It means God-Damned Independents," said Bret.

"I'm a GDI," Caitlin said, smiling.

"Well, I don't know," said Bret. "You go to a different school." He finished his burger and crumpled up the wrapper.

"It's not that different," said Caitlin.

Bret kicked back in his chair and took a drag of soda. The sunlight flashed off his necklace.

"Oh," said Caitlin. "Come here." He leaned forward and she held the disc for a second before letting it go. "Did you ever figure that thing out?"

"Me?" said Bret. "No. I don't know anything about it. I was hoping someone else would."

A tall guy boarded right past their table, taking the slope down toward Krasner Auditorium, wheels rattling on the pavement.

Caitlin stood up. "Well, I still don't," she said. "But I bet you could find out if you really tried." She picked up the tray with her barely touched salad.

Bret got up too. "Masters says it's kinda whack and I should maybe toss it," he said.

"He's just jealous 'cause he doesn't have one," said Caitlin, laughing. "Where do we dump these things?"

"Inside," said Bret. They walked into coolness.

Despite what Caitlin said, Bret had no idea how to figure out his incomprehensible disc of twisting glyphs, rising and setting suns. He guessed he'd keep asking around.

10

Bret hadn't asked her anything, but this girl with a blue cup was telling him anyway.

"Oh, my God, it so sucks to have mono," she was saying as they stood in the house backyard.

"Uh-huh," said Bret.

"Like, have you had mono," she asked, exhaling smoke.

"Yeah, once," said Bret. The girl had light brown hair and she looked really familiar.

"In the beginning it was really cool because I lost like ten pounds," the girl continued. "But then everyone's like, 'Oh, my God, she lost ten pounds, I totally need mono too.' You know?"

"Uh-huh," said Bret.

"So they'd like bring me sodas and stuff, and I was like, 'Thank you, that's so sweet,' but I'd have *one sip* and they'd just grab the can away from me and fight over who got to drink out of it next."

"Huh," said Bret.

"Some of the girls were like, 'We're gonna kiss you,' and they kept trying to get their tongues in my mouth. They were really aggro and it got really annoying. You know?" She took a long drag off her cigarette.

"Uh-huh," said Bret.

"And you just feel all sick and tired and stuff. Like I don't know if you remember back when the water polo team made sushi and like we all got hepatitis? But it's almost as bad as that." She reflected on the beer sloshing around in her blue cup.

"Was I talking to you before," Bret asked. "Your name's Tracy, right?"

The girl stared at him.

One of the pledges stuck his head out the door, panting, face flushed. "We got a Fiji," he gasped.

"Shit, where," asked Bret.

"In the kitchen," said the pledge, and pulled his head back into the darkness where colors flashed.

"Later," said Bret to the girl.

"Wait, what's going on," she asked, but Bret was already inside, back in the heat and the tangle of bodies and pounding music, pushing through the thicket of pastel spaghetti tanks and retro-eighties slogan shirts, heaving aside sweaty backs as he forced his way to the wooden door at the back of the room.

Then he was standing in the house kitchen. Industrial-grade appliances to feed seventy-nine. Four guys, pledges, stood in a loose circle around two guys who were holding some kid down on the white floor tiles.

They turned briefly when Bret came in. "This guy's a Fiji," Bret asked.

"Yeah," said one of the pledges. "Little Fiji fucker."

The kid tried to speak. A pledge kicked him and said, "Shut the fuck up, you little Fiji faggot."

"What should we do with him," asked another pledge.

"Whatever you want," said Bret. He sat on a chrome countertop and watched as they:

• Stripped the guy down to his boxers;

• Duct-taped his hands together and his feet together and then wrapped duct tape around his mouth;

(It was the week before Hell Week and pledges had the dual duty of going on missions to mess up the other fraternities while also protecting their own houses from invasion.)

• Got a black Sharpie marker and chiefed all over the guy, writing I AM A FAG!!! BLOW JOBS 25¢!! I SUCK FIJI COCK!! and drawing penises all over his face and his body;

• Kicked him a bunch.

(What with their war and all, you could say Fiji and PAK were—yeah—kinda rivals.)

Then they:

- Shaved the guy's head with an electric razor;
- Dumped trash from the garbage can on him;
- Poured out the dishwasher grease trap on him;
- Kicked him a bunch more for good measure.

(You had to show them that the mighty Pi Alpha Kappa knew how to represent.)

And then they:

- Stepped on his face;
- Pissed all over him;
- Kicked him really hard.

"Hey," said Bret.

The pledges turned. They were breathing heavily and their eyes were shining and they were smiling and laughing and joking around. "Yeah?" one of them said.

Bret felt bad because he didn't know why he had said "hey" and broken the moment and interrupted everyone from having a good time. It had just sort of happened. So to cover his confusion, he said, "Yo, I gotta do some birthday shots here."

"Oh, yeah!" one of his pledges said. "You're twenty-one!"

"Oh, happy birthday, man!" one of the other pledges said, wiping grease off his hand onto his jeans and then shaking Bret's hand a little apologetically. Other "happy birthdays!" floated around the group.

"Where've we got some hard A around here," Bret asked everybody.

"We used up most of it," one of the pledges said.

"Tolski has some in his room," another volunteered.

A pause. "And?" Bret said.

"Oh, my bad," said the pledge, and ran off to get it.

The other pledges looked down at the thing on the floor.

"Yeah, get him out of here," said Bret.

But no one wanted to touch him because he had been pissed on. They all called each other pussies but they still didn't touch him, until one of the pledges got gloves from the back of the kitchen. Then one of the other pledges kicked the thing sharply again, and then they dragged him out the back door to leave him three houses down on the Fiji lawn.

Bret sat alone on the chrome kitchen counter for a little while, looking at the cereal boxes on the shelf and whistling along softly to the bass line of the music in the other room. The chef had taped a note in black ink under the dial thermometer on a clamped-shut door: MARCO'S FREEZER! DO NOT TOUCH!!! The ink had gotten wet and run.

Then the door swung open and the pledge came back in with a bottle of cherry schnapps and a shot glass.

"That's all he had," said the pledge.

"Bullshit," laughed Bret. "Tolski is a bitch." The pledge didn't want to say anything because he knew he'd only get himself into trouble.

"Do you want it," asked the pledge.

"Shot's a shot," said Bret.

The pledge stepped over to him, carefully avoiding the mess on the kitchen floor.

"Even though this isn't really a shot," Bret continued.

The pledge hesitated.

"Oh, come on," Bret said. "And you're doing one too."

"Okay," said the pledge.

He did a shot and then Bret did a shot.

"Oh, that just like tasted really weird," said the pledge. "Can I have a chaser?"

"No," said Bret.

He slid off the table. He was going somewhere to play.

Bret was playing darts in the big triple when they heard the chanting begin outside.

We have the power! We have the right!

"Oh, Jesus, not this again," said A-Rod, looking up from the NCAA Final Four tournament.

The campus is ours! Take back the night!

"Kill me now," groaned Martinez. He had the brackets open in front of him from the house's basketball betting pool.

"What the fuck is it," asked Bret.

"Go take a look," said Martinez, and pointed to the balcony.

The chanting was getting louder. Take back the night! The time is here!

"Your turn," said Dwight, gathering his darts.

We will not be controlled by fear!

"One sec," said Bret. He went over to the balcony door and looked down.

A chanting phalanx was advancing along the Row, a couple hundred people holding candles. Flickering flames glittered in the darkness, a loud and mobile constellation passing between streetlamp light pools.

"They do this every fucking year," said Dwight.

Join together, free our lives!

The swarm was passing right outside the PAK house.

We will not be victimized!

"They walk up and down again for hours," Martinez said.

Bret went back and tossed a dart. Bull's-eye.

"Damn you," said Dwight.

Two-four-six-eight!

"How the hell did Gonzaga get to the tournament?" wondered A-Rod.

Your gender roles are woman hate!

"This is ruining my quality of life," said Martinez.

"Shut up!" yelled A-Rod from the futon.

Sexist, rapist, anti-gay . . .

"'Shut up' on three," said Martinez. "One, two, three—"

"Shut up!" they all yelled toward the balcony.

You can't take our night away!

"Dude," said Dwight, "we should like blast them back with the stereo."

"Yeah, dude!" said A-Rod. "Like play some really offensive song out the window."

Martinez was laughing. "Yeah, some gangsta shit or something."

"Aw, that would be hella funny," said Dwight.

Bret and Dwight kept tossing darts while Martinez and A-Rod decided on the Notorious B.I.G.'s "Big Booty Hoes" and got the file off the Internet.

"Prepare yourselves, my friends," announced Martinez, and he and Dwight turned the speakers around and put them out on the balcony. They cranked the volume to max and hit play as the candle group worked its way back past their house.

Hey, hey, ho, ho, sexual assault has got to—

Then the speakers cut in, mega-loud: "Yeayah! You didn't know that we be PISSIN' on hoes, biyatch!"

The chanting died out and everyone was laughing as Biggie laid down his own unique vision of gender roles.

"Could there possibly be a more offensive song?" marveled A-Rod, impressed.

"That is so fucking tight!" laughed Martinez.

There was some noise in the hall. Bret stuck his head out the door to investigate and saw three girls with candles marching down the second-floor corridor.

"Candle people are here," he gasped.

And then they were in the room, glaring at everybody and at the speakers on the balcony where Biggie rapped on, oblivious.

"That's really disrespectful," snapped one of the girls.

She was tall and had unbrushed blond hair pulled back with a red bandanna.

"We have free speech," said Martinez, shrugging.

A girl in blue coveralls curled a lip, her candle flame reflected in her square black glasses. "That's not free speech. That's hate speech," she said.

"That's Biggie's speech," said A-Rod. "You should go talk to him."

A small girl with light brown hair, very plain features, and a big nose stepped to the front. She looked familiar. "This is the worst house on the Row and you need to formally apologize to the community outside."

"You need to get off our property," said A-Rod. "You're trespassing."

The girl surveyed their faces and fixed her gaze on Bret. "You. You're in my grade and you're in my econ class. Ask your frat brothers to apologize."

Bret laughed nervously. "Well?" the girl demanded.

"What do you mean, we're the worst house on the Row?" said A-Rod. "What the fuck do you know about our house?"

The girl spun around to face him. "I know a lot about your house. I'm Emma Haviland."

Dwight and A-Rod and Martinez suddenly looked at each other.

"My brother Miller was your President for two years and I've been coming here since I was twelve," said the girl. "I *was beer bonging with the PAKs while you were trading Pogs, but I grew up."*

A long pause before A-Rod spoke. "Look, just don't bother—"

Emma cut him off. "I'm marching because your house assaulted my friend Jessica Keating and nothing was resolved, and now you're insulting her more with that music."

Martinez laughed without smiling. "Yeah, we've already fought a war with Fiji about that, thanks."

"The Fijis have nothing to do—," Emma started.

Martinez pointed to each one of the guys. "Okay, and I have nothing to do with it, Adrian has nothing to do with it, Dwight has nothing to do with it, and our pledge has nothing to do with it. First, get out of my room, and if you have a problem, go bitch to the paper like everyone else."

Emma stared at him. But Bret had been looking at the girl with square glasses. "Wait," he said. "Didn't you rush Alpha Chi Omega?"

The other girls turned to look at her. "Huh," she asked.

"No, you totally did," said Bret. "Your name is Linda or something. I remember they were talking about you at dinner. You didn't get a bid."

Linda and Bret stood unmoving for a while. Then she held out her arm.

"Oops," she said, and dropped her candle into a heap of papers by the door.

"You fucking bitch!" screamed Martinez as the flames sprang up, and the three girls disappeared and everybody scrambled to put out the blaze. As he saw the fire rising Bret couldn't hide a quick shudder.

11

The wooden table shook with the force of Bret's winning goal. "Oh my God, so he's like famous," a voice was saying behind him.

Back in the side room, the beer pong board was off to reveal foosball, in which Bret had just kicked Ryan Yeagermeister's ass. He turned away from the table to see two girls frozen in a posture of mild embarrassment.

"Hey, Bret!" said the one dressed in pale blue. "I was just telling my little sib about how you were on the reality thing last year."

"That's *so* cool!" added a cuter one wearing pale pink and holding a premium-grade red cup.

"What's your name again," Bret asked the blue one, who had a blue cup. Slightly lower quality.

She glanced briefly at the pink one. "I'm Christa,

remember? Carolyn's my roommate and you went with her to our semi."

"Yeah, I guess," said Bret. "You're Alpha Phis?"

"Uh-huh!" Christa pushed the pink girl forward. God, she wasn't actually wearing *glitter,* was she? "This is my little sib, Amanda."

"What's up, Amanda," said Bret.

Amanda stared at Bret, wide-eyed. "So like, were the cameras on you twenty-four-seven?"

"I love your hat," Christa told Yeagermeister. It was shaped like a giant condom.

"Yeah," said Bret.

"How did they pick y'all," Amanda asked. "I bet like everyone wanted to do it."

"Thanks," said Yeagermeister. He took the hat off and showed it to her.

"I guess they decided we could party," Bret told Amanda, looking over her head for someone else to talk to.

"So was it, like, really cool being a celebrity?"

Bret thought for a second. "It sucked." He paused. "Oh, man, I probably gotta do another shot. Great meeting you."

Voices followed him as he walked away. "Yeah, he was like the craziest one, too. He was like hang-gliding drunk and he almost killed himself."

"He's *so* cute. . . ."

And then the house music drowned them out. Remix of

a remix, words repeated, broken up. *"If you want to move the world, start with your body."*

Bret traveled east down the hallway. He ran his hand along the wood paneling to keep balance. Rows of old chapter composite photos dating back to 1934 stared down at him. Bret wondered how many of those slick-haired kids had died by now. He wondered if the house had ghosts.

The hallway was narrow. Bret stepped over a pair of cargo pants and a green cup by the tweed couch where some guy wearing an Adidas visor straddled this girl Bret had gone out with sophomore year. Her eye caught Bret's and he pointed at her and laughed.

Steady streams of people moved up and down the side stairway. Marty jumped off the bottom step and said, "There's a crew up on the balcony."

"Right on," said Bret. He climbed.

Down the hall he passed Tolski's open door where the TV was talking to an empty room. "—the Department of Homeland Security has likewise unveiled its Total Information Awareness Program, which officials say will allow the Defense—"

Bret walked into and through the big triple where the bright lights were out and the blacklights made the white on his shirt glow. He climbed out the window. The balcony curved around the front and side of the PAK house. Five years ago they had an incident with the iron railing that kinda ended up bad.

Stevens, two pledges, and some random chicks were leaning against the rail. Stevens wore a huge sombrero. Everyone with a cup had a red one. "Whassup, boys," Bret said.

"Eees *Señor Veintiuno!*" The snap. "Have a beeer, *señor,*" said Stevens.

Bret grabbed a Sierra Nevada from the cooler.

"Ay ay ay ay ay," Stevens was saying. He was massaging the neck of one of the random girls.

"Keeping the theme alive, huh," said Bret.

"I'm still Running for the fucking Border, *vato,*" said Stevens. "And the dean can suck it."

Bad placement: down and out from the side balcony stretched the cool concrete-glass buildings of the Technology Quad. The university had built those crystal installations right across the street from the end of the Row.

The massaged girl was giggling now. "Ooh, ooh! Look at the little freaks! Aren't they adorable?"

"I want to punch those fuckers," said one of the pledges. *"Bam!"*

The house cast a big shadow because of the streetlamps behind it, so it was hard to see the three guys walking out of the Tech Quad. Bret knew they sucked because they had that kinda hunched-over walk, pulled back by huge backpacks, more running than walking really, not wanting to stand too long in the same place. A nerdy power-walk, arms dangling limply at their sides, necks stretched forward, their whooping laughs drowned by pounding house music. One fat one, waddling along.

"Yo, faggots!" Stevens screamed off the balcony.

A couple of them glanced up briefly at the house.

"Hey, we're talking to you, you gay-ass pieces of shit!" Bret bellowed.

Maybe they walked faster. The random girls were laughing. "You have to get trashed tonight," one of them shrieked.

"We have beer!" Stevens added, holding up a bottle of Sierra Nevada. "Probably don't like it though. Fuckin' find some dicks."

The geeks stopped, seemed to be conferring. Then they turned around and called out in reedy unison, hands cupped around their mouths: *"That's all right! It's okay! You'll all work for us one day!"*

They raised their middle fingers and loped off awkwardly. You could hear the giggles now.

"Fuckin' A!" screamed Stevens. Bret turned to see Stevens was gritting his teeth as he threw the beer bottle as hard as he could across the street, but it missed the geeks completely and exploded with a pop and a shatter, a storm of fragments in the middle of the road.

The letters fragmented, danced, and rejoined on his screen, repeating the same short message a thousand ways: GAME OVER. *Bret would play this old computer game after school in his father's study while Martina was off scrubbing somewhere and his parents were at work. It was called* Infinity Quest *and it sucked. You'd move this guy with a sword through all these different levels and after a while he'd die, like a rock would fall on him or a crocodile would shoot him. There was never any real progression in the game, just more things to fight and jump over. There wasn't a score either, unless maybe you counted that you could pick up bags of gold—a whole lot of them if you really tried—which you could trade in for items (like a jet pack) by pressing the space bar. You could take lots of different paths through interesting scenery, but whatever you bought and whichever way you went turned out essentially useless, because eventually the guy would just die a different way (for example, in a pit of acid). Bret spent forever at it, almost obsessively restarting, but he couldn't figure out the point and he junked the game when they moved. Every now and then he had a nightmare, though, of that little character dancing alone through repetitive and endless levels. He would wake gasping, his insides knotted.*

12

Stevens was still seething. One of the random girls stood behind him, her arms around his waist.

It was definitely bad placement to put the Technology Quad so close to the Row, but the university was shutting down houses right and left now anyway.

Stevens leaned hard on the iron rail. His sombrero hung behind his head on its string. He stared at the metal and eventually had to mention the incident with Brother Russ Turner who supposedly had a memorial somewhere at PAK National. Bret had heard the story lots before and it kind of bored him, so he climbed back in the window and walked through the big blacklight triple to the hall.

The corridor had cleared out a bit and Bret only had to push past a few people. In the middle by the big stairs he stepped over a busted vacuum cleaner lying on its side, red cloth bag torn open, spilling dust.

The door to his room stood ajar. Inside, Jordan and a couple of guys Bret had never seen before were doing lines of coke off the silver mirrored cover of Bret's business ethics textbook.

"Bret Stanton!" said Jordan.

"What up," said Bret. They did the snap.

There was lots of speculation among business majors that the book cover was an in-joke by and for MBAs. A girl in Bret's section actually wrote to the author's e-mail address at four o'clock one Saturday morning demanding to know if it was true, but the message bounced.

"This guy is so awesome today!" said Jordan. "You know why this guy is so fucking awesome today?"

"Why are you so awesome today," one of the guys asked Bret.

"It's this stud's twenty-first birthday!" said Jordan.

Bret looked at the answering machine but the red light wasn't flashing.

"Yeah," one of the guys asked.

"He's getting old like me," said Jordan.

Bret did the snap with the random guys. They were sitting on Jordan's bed; Jordan on Bret's bed. Passing the textbook.

"Congratulations, bro," a guy said.

"Thanks, man," said Bret.

A playlist of gangsta rap MP3s thumping on desk speakers.

"But this guy, this guy," said Jordan, "is fucking awesome in two ways."

He held up two fingers so everyone understood.

"How else are you awesome," asked one of the random guys.

". . . *superstar. That is what you are. Coming from afar. Reaching for the stars.* . . ."

"Old skool," the other guy laughed.

"Yeah, fuck this," said Jordan, reaching over and clicking. The song changed. "This guy is also awesome because he has a kick-ass job lined up with his dad when he graduates, and I cannot even consultate."

"Oh, yeah," asked one of the random guys.

"I don't know if I'm that into it," said Bret, trying to find the bottle of gin.

"What are you talking about," asked Jordan. "Dude, people would kill to get that."

Bret was looking under the desk where he saw a tangle of dusty wires.

"I mean, you're gonna be like on a *track*," Jordan was saying. "You're gonna make *bank*."

One of the guys noisily sucked up a line and shook his head to clear it. "Hurts so *good*!" he said. People were shouting out in the hall.

"So I can buy good coke, right, Jordan," asked Bret from under the desk.

"But you gotta give it to me," said Jordan, tossing his Nerf football up and down. "I'll be the guy in like rags begging outside."

Bret stood up. "Where's the gin," he asked.

"Gin's here," said one of the random guys, passing him the bottle.

Bret slammed back a unit from a dirty Spearmint Rhino strip club shot glass. "Oh yeah, number twelve." He unscrewed a plastic bottle half-full with warm, flat Sprite and gulped a few mouthfuls.

"That's my boy," said Jordan, pretending to cry.

"You're doing twenty-one," one of the random guys asked.

"Yeah," said Bret.

"Good luck," laughed the guy.

Jordan was grooving to the beat. "Dude, I'm ready to fucking go dance," he said. "Get some slizutties. You getting play on the big two-one, Stants?"

"Yeah," said Bret. He pointed to where Jordan was sitting. "I had sex on that bed like less than an hour ago."

"No fucking way," said Jordan.

"Check the garbage can, homey," said Bret.

And they did and Jordan hopped up and was like, "I'm changing these pants," and the random guys were laughing and Bret laughed too, and he stepped out the door into the hallway, shaking his head.

o o o

Willens was shaking his head.

"No one can get in unless some fuckhead lets 'em in. So don't let 'em in."

He looked around the chapter room. No one said anything.

"Keep medical people outside the door. You may want to let 'em in if there's a problem, but don't. If they get inside, they can seriously fuck us up, with like underage drinking. Overfilling the house. Remember the Phi Kaps. We don't want Newsweek crawling around snapping pictures of everything.

"If someone's seriously messed, toss 'em outside ASAP. Otherwise, insurance goes up. Every death costs National three million. Y'all know this, I hope."

"That's it for Treasurer/Risk Management," he finished, saluting Masters. "Grand Officer."

Treasurer mattered. Risk Management ended up a kind of bonus bullshit position to put on the résumé.

Masters did the sign and Willens sat. Masters looked over the room slowly. "We're being attacked from every side," he said. "They're just looking for an opportunity to get us. I mean I don't care what you have to do: Don't let that happen. Think about how long we've been on campus. Think about how much this house means to your brothers. Remember the Phi Kaps."

A moment of silence. Masters smiled. "Social Committee," he said.

Kevin Whalen stood and saluted. "Okay! We're starting out the year strong. 'Anything for an A' went really well last night, and I think PAK did a good job welcoming all the new frosh to campus. Some of us did a really frighteningly good job. Reilly."

A bunch of guys said "Reilly" and tousled his hair and slapped him on the back. He smiled.

"I think the hot tub will never be safe again," said Kevin. "Anyway, a bunch of brothers said frosh guys were interested in pledging but missed Rush, so if you have names for spring, talk to this man over here." He pointed to Nate, who gave a little wave.

"Also," said Kevin, "make sure the pledges see the clean-up sheet, which is in the, uh—"

"First-floor hall," said Marty.

"First-floor hall," Kevin repeated. "Cool. That's it, Grand Officer." He saluted Masters. Grand Officer was the House President's formal title.

Masters stood up and looked at his watch. "A record. Thirty-four minutes. Good job, brothers." The purple robes of the President billowed as Masters intoned, "May PAK lead all who follow her path into light ever greater." He hit the gavel nine times.

"Hut! Break!" someone called out. People stood, did the handshake with their neighbors, and began to scatter.

Bret headed for the door. Craig was next to him. "Dude, I really think I'm gonna skip next time."

"Go for it," said Bret. "If you don't want fifty bucks, I'll take it."

"Fucking fines," said Craig.

Taylor McLaughlen ran over to Masters and said something. "Wait!" Masters called out. "Wait! We need more sign-ups for the tutoring thing!"

Guys heard and pushed out the door quickly.

"It's a really great thing to do," Masters was calling. "I sign up for a few kids every year."

Bret surged forward too, but he was toward the back and Taylor caught him and a few other people and made them pick time slots.

Since there was no hurry anymore, Bret stopped to tie his white Adidas sneaker. He was basically last in the room when he heard behind him, pretty quietly, "Hell."

Willens was sitting in the treasurer's chair, back to Bret. His robes glowed a grimy off-white in dirty sunlight that crept around the heavy window shade. Masters, walking out, patted Bret solidly on the shoulder.

"Hell," Willens said again, louder. Bret walked toward him and the wooden floor creaked. They were alone.

"'Sup," Bret asked.

Willens jumped and kind of glared but also relaxed. "Shit, Bret."

As he turned around, he shoved a piece of paper over to cover another one where the number $587,510.47 had been highlighted in yellow.

"What's five hundred eighty-seven thousand, five hundred ten dollars and forty-seven cents," asked Bret.

"Shit, Bret. Shit." Willens rubbed his forehead.

"It's on your paper. What is it," Bret asked again.

Kind of sadly, kind of vaguely, Willens looked at Bret. "What are you? A sophomore?"

"I'm a junior," said Bret.

"Right. Right, I knew that." Distantly. "You thinking about officer board next year?"

Bret kinda shrugged.

"You'll probably be on officer board, huh . . . ," Willens said.

Bret shrugged again.

"If I tell you something, you're not talking about it to anyone but Masters, or I will personally fuck you up."

"Um, okay."

The handshake while Bret swore.

"That's what we owe. We owe five hundred eighty-seven thousand dollars." Bret didn't answer and Willens continued: "That's the house debt."

Bret looked up at the ceiling fan and for the first time noticed—while Willens went on to say that for twelve years debt had grown, and really only Treasurers and Presidents knew—that each wooden blade had a picture of the sun in a different position.

He tried not to, but he thought of his medallion while Willens said alumni don't want to know, we don't tell. To distract himself from all kinds of things, his eyes tracked downward, following the line of the fan's cord along the wall. Instead of a clean switch, it ended with a hideous, intestinal burst of tangled wiring. That was really shocking, that was really sad.

Willens was looking at him, and Bret said, stomach twisting and sinking, "That sucks."

Willens kept looking at him.

"Why did you tell me that," Bret asked.

Willens laid his hands down on the pieces of paper. He looked at a fingernail.

"I guess I just wanted to tell somebody," he said eventually.

The wires looked very burned, corroded, black.

13

"Put on something black," Jesse said, grabbing Bret by the shoulder. He was carrying a big bundle. "Major PAK prank shit is going down to*night*!"

"What?" said Bret. "Like FUBU gear, puffy North Face?"

"No, fucker," laughed Jesse, as he swung toward the stairway. "Downstairs. We're out in three minutes."

In his room Bret gulped a painful shot of the harsh-ass gin. Number thirteen, classic. He almost gagged.

And with half a minute to spare, wearing a black hoodie and black windpants (white stripes, though) that he pulled on over his jeans, he shoved through the masses of bodies pressing into the doorway.

K-Money was standing on the porch. "Happy birthday," he said, smirking. "Have some high school chick's cell phone."

"Um, okay," said Bret. He shrugged and pocketed the little piece of plastic.

Free of the crowd, he saw a group of guys who didn't have invites laughing and shoving sticks into the utility box on the telephone pole outside.

"Hey!" yelled Bret, stopping. "What the fuck?"

Beeeeeep! He turned. A golf cart idled at the curb, Jesse behind the wheel, Rob next to him with the bundle in his lap. J.P. and Marty were cracking up about something in the backseat.

Jesse was calling, "Yo, Bret, get on!" The electric motor started to whine, and the cart jerked forward. Bret leaped up onto the back platform and gripped the aluminum poles.

Rob explained the plan.

Rob had twisted his ankle a couple of weeks ago in tennis and the school had lent him a golf cart.

Pretty badass.

J.P. and Marty couldn't fucking believe it.

The cart was zipping along the street. A cool, damp wind enveloped Bret, almost messing up his gelled hair.

Some of the guys had found this big PAK banner from a couple of years ago (maybe Greek Olympics). The banner said YOU COULDN'T COME TO OUR PARTY, BUT YOUR GIRLFRIEND CAME TWICE! Apparently there was also some funny cartoon, but no one could really remember what it looked like.

The pounding house music faded into the distance. Shadowy trees blurred past Bret.

A car streaked by, its wailing honk Dopplering away.

They were going to hang the banner from the observation deck of Ubermann Needle, a massive deco tower by the center of campus. It would be really sweet because they were having such a kick-ass party that night.

Bret laughed. The sophomores were about to piss themselves with excitement. Shit, yeah!

Lots and lots of wind. Going up and down surfaces. The cart swerved a few times, hit corners sharply.

Jesse slowed down as they got closer. They were driving through Rice Quad, big darkened buildings, sodium lampposts throwing sharp shadows.

Directly in front, bathed in harsh white floodlight, the Needle's bleak mass peaked twenty stories high.

They parked around the corner, where its immense shadow gave better cover. Bret jumped down off the back of the cart.

"Grab the banner," Jesse told the sophomores. He and Rob climbed out.

"Comfy back there," he asked Bret.

Bret shrugged. "Your mom was a better ride."

"What? What?" said Jesse, mock stepping.

J.P. was looking up at the Needle. "How the fuck are we supposed to get in," he asked.

"Dude, I'm not thinking *that* far," Rob said. They walked around to the front and stopped by the massive brass doors, which were covered in endlessly interlocking triangles that reflected a crazy geometric pattern onto the ground. Bret looked down. He stood on top of a big carved 1936.

VBERMANN TOWER was deeply etched into stone above the great doorway. Two hulking statues—stylized, a boy and a girl—flanked it, hands locked downward at their sides, expressionless faces gazing upward at twin floodlights over their heads.

TO THE, read the boy's plinth.

STUDENT, read the girl's plinth.

"Fuckin' A," said Jesse. He put his hands on his hips and looked pissed off.

"There's got to be *something*," said Rob. He started off around the other side of the Needle.

Where they found a little wooden door with a padlock on it behind the low shrubs. Some letters had been stenciled on peeling paint, but they were too faded to read.

Rob started kicking it, ninja style. He had been a yellow belt in karate. Marty picked up a big rock and tried to smash it in. J.P. got a beer from the golf cart and sat on the rolled-up banner and watched them.

Bret couldn't think of much to do, so he was the first to see the flashlight and the rent-a-cop watching them, saying into his walkie-talkie, "Left service door. I see five here. Breaking and entering."

"Break!" screamed Bret, and saw the other guys flipping out, spinning around. He just ran for it, going superfast like you always do when you're buzzing. Pounding past the trees, hearing the walkie-talkie behind him, running, running . . .

Bret exhaled measured clouds of fog through his nose as his cleats pounded the grass blades sharpened by frost.

"You don't like running goalposts?" Coach Mathy bellowed through a megaphone somewhere far behind them. "Randolph's running goalposts. Bet your ass they are."

Bret pounded along in silence. Around him a flock of red bodies, helmets streaked with white. They were all breathing fog.

"Let's get moving! Let's hustle! This isn't stadiums."

Behind the far goalposts rose the scoreboard. WOOD-BRIDGE CENTRAL HIGH SCHOOL. AXEMEN 00. VISITOR 00. Bret briefly clenched his mouth guard between his teeth and then relaxed his jaw.

The megaphone barked: "Let's finish off this season like winners. Hustle! Hustle!"

They reached the goalposts. Only whistling wind and the crunch of grass out here. Bret and his flock banked, restraightened, pounded back toward the other set of posts.

"Lopez, get up there!"

Bret's feet fell rhythmically. He was a red jersey among red jerseys. A little beyond the coming goalposts, a path led off into the distance.

The mechanical voice rose and fell, a distant but constant irritant: "Atkins! Strideman! You playing around back there? Come on. Move!"

Bret had no idea where the path went. He could see it cut across the broad fields of high grass that lay behind the stadium. After that it might plunge into woods. Maybe it continued through the low rolling hills that chained off beneath a slate sky of fast-moving clouds.

"You're gonna let Randolph wipe the field with you! They're gonna feel sorry for the Axemen."

If Bret didn't bank when the rest of the flock did, he could just keep going straight and run right on ahead down that path to whatever distant lands it coursed.

"Hustle!"

The goalposts were right ahead of them.

"Hustle!"

Once Bret saw a deer in the high grass.

"HUSTLE!"

They reached the goalposts, and the flock banked. Bret banked too, although he staggered for a millimeter and was slightly off step. The flock restraightened.

They pounded back toward Coach Mathy.

Bret would have been kicked off the team. He would have had to give up his letter jacket. He wouldn't have known what to do when he went in to school, who he would sit with. That path had very serious consequences.

All around Bret a flock of red bodies ran, helmets streaked with white.

White lights in the night, flash of the searching light beam.

Bret dashed breakneck through an open area of cement path. A dark building rested in silence, partially shadowed from the sodium lamps. Surrounded by hedges. Bret collapsed into the bushes and curled up on dirt, pressed against the wall of the building, lungs burning, heart thudding.

Officers were walking by. Voices of authority, crackles of static. They wanted to lock him up and stop motion.

The leaves scratched Bret's face. A big spiderweb glistened between two clawlike branches.

The ground was cool and soft. Bret dug his fingers into the dirt and tried to push farther back against the wall of the building.

He waited. Through the bushes, the path looked empty.

Then the cell phone rang, playing—high and chirpy— the chorus of some damned Justin Timberlake song.

"Shit, shit, shit," Bret hissed, fumbling around in the pocket of his windpants, not finding the phone, then clawing at his jeans underneath.

He snagged the phone and pulled it out, stared at it. It was very small indeed. *How the hell do you turn this one off?*

He thought he heard walkie-talkies returning in the distance. He snapped the phone open. The display had been wrecked, liquid crystal blobs slid over glowing blue. He had probably crushed it somehow.

He found the button to reject a call. Timberlake fell silent.

He waited, trying to breathe shallowly, as quietly as possible. The glowing blobs shifted. The footsteps and voices sounded more distant.

Then Justin Timberlake started up again.

Bret winced, hit the pick-up button, and held the phone to his ear.

"Hello?!" a voice was saying. "Jenna, it's Lizzie. Are you, like, getting some action or what?" There were some giggles in the background.

"Listen, you gotta stop calling this phone," whispered Bret.

A moment of silence. The voice more distant: "Oh my *God,* Jenna's hooking up with a college guy."

"Oh my *God*!" A group of faint, excited shrieks, babble of voices that cut in and out. "He's like on the phone. . . ."

Bret leaned his head against the cool, rough concrete blocks behind him. They scratched his neck and pressed into his scalp.

Now the voice came back, loud. "Hello, college guy?"

"Hi," said Bret.

"Can we talk to Jenna?"

"No," said Bret.

Pause. "What?"

Bret took a deep breath. "You really can't. I have no idea who the fuck she is."

He pressed the red hang-up button.

The phone stayed silent. Distantly Bret heard a car drive away.

He rose slowly against the wall and began to move. Vulnerable, uncovered.

Cover off, bass pumping, Bret drove his black Jeep Wrangler past the big white sign painted blue that welcomed him to the Gold Coast Shopping Plaza.

Bret's mom and dad were at a stalemate in their endless war against each other. The new gambit was that both refused to pay for anything. Each was waiting for the other to crack, and chances were looking ever slimmer that Bret would get any money for spring quarter dues or even tuition.

He needed cash bad. He parked in the glint of hot sunlight reflecting off the other car colors, cherry reds, ocean metallics, and AA yellows.

The mall was glass panes stretched across a white pipe trellis. Cold air blasted Bret when he opened the door. Inside, the floor gleamed, faint R&B played on the speaker system, and stores stretched away for three levels on both sides of a central aisle of tall palm trees and glossy lacquered benches. A few people, mainly vacant-eyed women with leaping kids, moved idly down the gallery.

Bret stepped inside the Pacific Outfitters store where the music was colder, almost a trance beat. Giant pictures of Pacific Outfitters guys and girls hung from the walls among skimboards and lacrosse sticks. Some teenagers were wandering around and poking through the racks. A guy maybe a few years older than Bret leaned against the counter with his head kinda cocked back.

"Hey, what's up," said Bret.

"What's up," the guy said.

"I'm looking for a job," said Bret. "And Jesse Gavin from my fraternity said I should check you guys out."

"Oh, yeah, Jess," said the guy. "Cool. What's your name?"

Bret told him. The guy said he was Logan and they shook hands.

Logan looked Bret up and down.

"Okay, Bret," he said. "Let me tell you something."

Bret waited to hear what it was. Logan leaned his arm on the counter and looked down for inspiration.

"The most important part of Pacific Outfitters," Logan said finally, "is the Pacific Outfitters Lifestyle."

"Uh-huh," said Bret, listening.

"The Pacific Outfitters Lifestyle is fun, easygoing, laid back. But cool, you know? Really cool. It's prep but it's surfer. It's a prep-surfer crossover. It's party, it's chill, it's all-American, it's always looking great."

Logan paused, and looked Bret up and down very slowly. At last he spoke. "I think you may have the Pacific Outfitters look."

He fixed Bret with gray eyes. "But do you have the Pacific Outfitters Lifestyle?"

Bret thought and then nodded. "I think so," he said.

Logan's gaze was steady, unbreaking. Long pause. "Well, you said you were in a fraternity, which is good. And you know Jess, and he's pretty close to living the Lifestyle." He tapped the counter. "Yeah, I'll give you a shot."

"Sweet," said Bret.

He filled out some paperwork. Logan looked it over and apparently decided it all checked out. He looked at his watch. "You know, I could actually use you to start right now," he said. "Can you start right now?"

"Sure," said Bret.

Logan pointed to a silver square on the floor by the entrance. "We're about to hit the big after-school crowd," he said. "So I need a Lifestyle Representative to stand there."

Bret looked at the silver square. It was about two feet across. "Just stand there," he asked.

"Yeah," said Logan. He reached behind the counter and tossed Bret a water polo ball. "Do you play water polo," he asked.

"Sometimes," said Bret.

"But you're not on the team," he asked.

"No," said Bret.

"That's too bad," said Logan. "Oh, well. Put on your sunglasses and go stand on the square. Look cool. Look popular. Live the Lifestyle, Bret. Let everyone see you're living the Lifestyle."

"Okay," said Bret.

He put on his sunglasses and held the water polo ball and walked over and stood in the silver square.

Soon high school kids started to trickle in, and Bret practiced looking cool and looking popular and showing everyone that he was living the Pacific Outfitters Lifestyle. After a while he decided that meant kinda cocking his head back and vaguely swinging the water polo ball around in a slightly aggressive yet chill way, and when some girl pretended she wasn't looking but actually was to do some quick hot-dogging move with the ball like he was having fun with it. If a girl actually looked at him for a while, he would kinda smile at her and then just toss the ball up in the air easy and catch it. The guys glanced at him in a totally threatened manner and bought more clothes.

That was Bret's job, although it turned out he didn't have to pay for spring quarter after all. A few weeks later his dad gave in and began to foot the bills again.

Bret quit, but soon found he missed work. Whenever he felt confused, like he might not be doing the right thing, he would just remember the time the Western Seaboard Division Manager of Pacific Outfitters came for his bimonthly visit to line up all the Lifestyle Representatives and rate them aloud on a scale of one to ten. He gave Bret a nine. The highest score, separating him from the pack.

14

Bret separated himself from the bushes and took a couple of steps into a little clearing to the west of Rice Quad. He turned around under the black iron light poles. The poles were everywhere. Frederickson, one of the football guys who graduated the year before, used to get wired on speed or coke and shake them. The glass globes would fall off the top and Frederickson would leap back and they would smash on the ground. Frederickson really seemed to hate the lampposts and as soon as he got fucked up he would head straight for them to do battle. One night he took out like eighty-four of them.

Bret could orient himself because east was always easy to find: The great fairy wing of a parabolic dish craned toward the heavens above the Punto Nitido National Observatory on the highest summit of the eastern hills. The

PAK house was the opposite way. Bret wanted to go home and walked west.

But around the corner stood a policeman.

Staring into blackness by a light pole, that tense uniformed body began to turn around, to find, catch, imprison Bret. Beginning to pivot, irises constricting, readying to locate him . . .

Bret's hands clenched and he prepared to dive back into the cover of the bushes.

Then: *Ka-BAM! BOOOM!* Golden fireworks ripped away the night. Huge, massive explosions took up the whole heavens, sunburst clouds of gold and white, immense storms of light, flickering pixilated points streaking and falling in a digital shower against blackness. They lit up the clearing like day, throwing all the bushes and lampposts into stark relief.

Bret gasped to find himself in a world of universal light, pinned in the open, exposed in brightness from all angles. He looked around, frantic, finding no safety, no exit, all warm darkness ripped away. He trembled in panic.

But the policeman was looking up too, transfixed by the starbursts drifting down above him.

BLAM! Ka-POW!

Cannon-crack booms, apocalyptic roaring. The rain of digital gold exploding above him and around him, Bret a tiny figure running away under a storm of brilliance, his shadow erased.

He tore down empty stone walkways that threaded between the monolithic buildings of Rice Quad. Firework booms echoed and reechoed down the canyons of stone walls. He didn't dare look behind.

Soon the thunder faded together with the eerie glow of lights exploding in the sky. He slowed to a jog and then just stopped, legs cramping and breathing ragged. He peered around the corner into an open-air arcade off the side of the Quad, a square of rough bricks fitted together mission-style.

Hundreds of people at tables and a stage filled the space. No policemen anywhere. A catering van parked off to the side, all objects lit by nine light trees that Event Services had set up.

Tall black speakers framed the stage. A man with white hair and glasses was saying into a microphone, "For closing remarks, it gives me immense pleasure to introduce University President Deandra Romapella!"

The man clapped big and stepped aside as the people at the tables clapped too. A large white banner read PONIENTE ALUMNI ASSOCIATION WELCOMES YOU BACK!

A woman stepped up to the microphone, her gray hair elaborately styled. She wore a white suit and what looked like a gold pin that caught rays from the light trees.

"Thank you, Jim," she said, turning back to look at him. Her voice was kinda nasal and it echoed piercingly off the L-shaped wall behind Bret. "Really, Jim and the Alumni

Association have done a tremendous amount of work, so let's give them some applause too."

More clapping. Bret moved right near to the tables that filled the arcade. Since all the lights pointed inward, no one could see him in the darkness.

University President Deandra Romapella took a sip of water and surveyed the crowd. "One of the fundamental challenges of the university," she began, "is to define its own role in society. This challenge is so important because society and the university are joined together like parent and child. I'm sure you're aware that nothing happens in the world at large—no trend, movement, or idea—that doesn't impact us here. Quite clearly it's a mutual relationship; as goes the university, so goes the nation. Those of you who remember the sixties probably understand the strength of this relationship better than anyone." Laughter.

"There is no so-called Ivory Tower, but we do have a very nice Needle that I hope you'll take the time to revisit this weekend." Predictable laughter. Now Bret stood next to a light tree behind the tables. Hundreds of now-cleared place settings, dozens of bottles of wine, golden center-pieces. There was a fat guy sitting right in front of Bret who was drinking his wine.

"We're not the real world," said President Romapella, "but we're the real world writ small. That's what the word 'university' means: We're a little universe. And so one of the questions we ask ourselves is, how does our little universe fit in the big one, how can we produce *graduates* who will not only fulfill a meaningful role in today's society but also work to shape the world of tomorrow? For a number of years, we at Poniente have had somewhat of a struggle with this process of self-definition."

She chuckled, and a number of alums chuckled because she was chuckling. The chubby guy in front of Bret smiled halfheartedly. Bret realized he had never seen Romapella in person except for one day during First-Year Orientation and once on the field at a football game.

"Unfortunately we arrived at the match a little late," she continued, "compared to some of the other schools we began competing with. The L.A. market, which is primarily the entertainment industry and its related services, already found itself under something of a lockdown by certain schools which will remain nameless."

She whispered into the mike, "USC and UCLA." Then she covered her mouth and tittered conspiratorially. The alumni joined in. Some, like the chubby guy, nodded. Bret scanned their faces. White hair, brown hair: mix of ages.

Romapella took another sip of water. "But now it appears that, thanks to the enormous generosity of its alumnae and alumni, Poniente may finally have found the direction it was looking for. Completed three years ago—at the cost of a hundred million dollars—our Technology Quadrangle began to prepare the next generation of Poniente students for a lifetime of achievement."

Tumultuous applause. Okay, the chubby guy looked familiar. Like Miller Haviland plus thirty to forty pounds, maybe.

"The generous support of our alumni has enabled us to leap over Los Angeles entirely and plug directly into the growing technology-driven economies of San Diego and Orange County. Our effort toward this goal has also been aided considerably by some fundamental rebudgeting," Romapella said.

More applause. "Miller," Bret whispered.

"Now the students of Poniente are going to be even more fortunate," Romapella said.

"Miller," Bret whispered more loudly. A few people shot him dirty looks.

Romapella lifted a hand and made a sweeping gesture. "Once our current giving campaign is finished, we'll be able to expand the Quad to twice its present size and build a number of additional new facilities!"

"Miller," said Bret. Lots of glares, someone shushed him. And the chubby guy turned around and stared.

Miller Haviland, the original PAK legend. Grand Officer the year before Bret arrived. Also a Fraternity Man of the Year.

"So on behalf of the students of Poniente University, present and future, I want to thank you all sincerely for your participation in the campaign." President Deandra Romapella smiled and clasped her hands. "We're going to conclude with some more fireworks in just a little while. Right now, dessert is served, so let's eat, drink, and be merry!" She left the stage in a flurry of applause. String music cut in on the speakers. Glasses clinked, a babble of voices began.

Bret stepped around the light tree into brightness. "Oh my God," said Miller Haviland, looking up at him. "It's, um . . ."

"Bret," said Bret. A few people from Haviland's table glanced over, but quickly went back to talking.

"Right," said Haviland. He shook his head. "Wow, I remember when you came to visit the house."

"Oh, yeah," said Bret.

"You really made an impression," Haviland said.

Bret smiled. "I had to represent for high schoolers."

Haviland shook his head again. "I guess you decided to come, huh? God, what year are you? Like a sophomore?"

"I'm a junior," said Bret. "I'm actually twenty-one today."

Haviland laughed. "No shit!" he said. "Happy birthday!"

"Yeah, I'm a PAK," said Bret. "I'm doing the twenty-one."

"Well, shit!" said Haviland. "You're a PAK?"

"Yeah, you guys convinced me," said Bret. They did the handshake.

"Come on," said Haviland. "Pull up a chair and sneak in here."

The string music played on and the glasses clinked. Bret slid into an empty place at Haviland's table. "Unless you're busy partying or whatever . . . ," Haviland said.

"I was just heading back to the house to finish my drinks," said Bret.

"Well, shit," said Haviland. "We've got stuff here." He poured Bret a glass of wine. "What are you on?"

Bret pointed at the glass. "That's fourteen."

Haviland laughed. "Fuck. Did you puke?"

"Nope," Bret said. He began to drink the wine.

The other six people at the table carefully kept their eyes pointed away except for a few tiny glances. "See," said Haviland. "No one cares you're here. I'm just sneaking everyone in tonight."

"Oh yeah," asked Bret.

"Yeah, I had my sister here too," said Haviland. "I told her she could get a real meal for once."

Bret blinked.

"You're in her spot," said Haviland. "She got a phone call and ran off."

Bret shifted in his chair.

"Miller," he said, "she's obsessed. She wants to destroy our house."

Haviland chuckled. "I'm surprised the house lasted this long. We thought they were going to take it away years ago."

Bret gaped. "You did?"

Haviland looked almost puzzled. "Well, yeah. I mean,

so much of the stuff is kinda on the edge, you know?"

A caterer walked by with big silver trays of desserts.

"I heard tonight I'm probably going to be Fraternity Man of the Year," said Bret. "Like you."

Miller looked confused for a second, and then he smiled. "Oh, God, yeah, I was. What were they thinking?" He laughed.

"It'll be in the chapter newsletter," said Bret.

"Shit, you mean now I have to read it," asked Miller.

"You don't read the newsletter," asked Bret.

Miller half-smiled as he reached for his glass.

Every table had a bouquet of white flowers in a golden vase at the center. "'The bonds of Pi Alpha Kappa unite men into an Eternal Brotherhood that extends far beyond their undergraduate years,'" recited Bret.

"When you decode that," said Miller, "it means PAK National keeps asking you for donations. Wait till you see the stuff you get in the mail."

Bret thought he saw the glint of a badge in the darkness beyond the light trees. He gulped his wine.

"Shit, it's a college thing, you know? It was fun, we had good times, I'd probably do it again. I don't know what more we're looking for."

Bret looked back at Miller. "You'd 'probably' do it again?" Okay, he thought he saw a dark hat, a uniform.

"I might, I might not. Shit, I don't know. I think it was right for me when I did it, you know?"

Okay, the guy was definitely a cop, and he was surveying the tables. Bret drained his glass of wine. "Thanks," he said. "I gotta go finish my drinks."

Miller reached out a big hand and they shook. "Good to see you again," he said, a wide grin on his fat face. "Say hi to the boys for me."

Bret stood. He couldn't tell if the cop was looking at him or not. The string music cut off. Someone was talking into the microphone, but Bret listened only to the crackling of a walkie-talkie in darkness.

He tossed off a little wave to Miller and dove beyond the light tree into an empty expanse of rough beige stone.

Stevens dove to catch the soccer ball he was bouncing off the side of the big metal freezer. The dishwasher roared softly as Evan leaned against the industrial mixer, eating a Hot Pocket.

"Where is that trick," Bret asked the room.

"Did you lose your chica," asked Tom Hunter.

"She was here like five seconds ago," said Bret.

"Check Frederickson's room." Evan laughed, hollering after Bret as he walked out across the empty common room. The TV was off, the sliding glass doors pushed back, and the front door propped open with a garbage can. Warm air blew through the space. A car drove past with music playing.

He walked down the side hall but it was empty, room

doors closed. A life-size cardboard cutout of Elvis looked suave, leaning against the wall next to the foosball table. Mike Michalek had proclaimed him eternal house mascot along with the dog. Bret climbed the side stairs.

On the second floor: most people off at lecture or section, a few upperclass guys watched him suspiciously as he passed open doors.

He went up again. The third-floor hall was empty except for a shiny upright vacuum cleaner with a cloth bag. It glinted gold in afternoon light from the hall windows. Lack of decoration and pervasive stillness: No one ever came up so far except the sophomores and unlucky juniors who lived here. A low beat behind the door that said SAM MASTERS.

Bret headed back down the main stairs. Voices coming from the barroom as he crossed the lounge. He stopped by the hall to listen.

"Yeah, he's tight," Masters was saying. "He's my little bro."

"Yeah," Caitlin was saying. "He really looks up to you. Like you have a really big influence on him."

"That's really cool," said Masters. "You guys went to like the same high school or something?"

"Uh-huh," said Caitlin. "In Massachusetts."

"Nice," said Masters. "Sorry, you know, he never like mentioned you or whatever."

Bret watched dust pass through the warm beams of golden light.

Caitlin laughed. "Well, I'm sure there's a lot of stuff going on here, and he's like way involved, huh?"

"Yeah," said Masters. The sound of the beer tap hissing. "Bret's real active in the house. The bid was a good fit for him."

"Oh," said Caitlin. "Yeah."

Bret wandered away. He looked out a window. It was really bright, and there were some guys goofing around in the yard. Panes of glass muffled their shouts.

The noise of tables and stage softening behind him, Bret hurried alone behind the massive hulking shapes of the buildings of the School of Humanities and Social Sciences. On a third floor he saw the darkened window where his econ section met.

Several lights still burned and he looked through glass to see a few pale forms working late at computers or poring over paper-clipped documents. Occasionally a back door would open and a shape would hurry off to the parking lot in silence and darkness.

Ka-BAANNG! BOOOOM!

The rough bricks rang with the force of the explosion. Fireworks flared again, white and gold showers pouring down, tossing the dark alley with sharp bursts of brightness.

Bret hurried along, the dish standing patient in the heavens behind him, his house far ahead.

BLAAAMMM! KA-POW!

The vast trails of light dazzled. You couldn't see for a few seconds after they fell.

KA-BANG! BLAAAMMM!

In the light of this vivid burst Bret saw the officer standing in front of him. He lowered his walkie-talkie for a second when he saw Bret and then quickly brought it up to his mouth again.

KA-POW! Little bits of mortar crumbled unseen from the old stone walls and the cop's outline flared. Bret started to run the other way and the cop was running after him, yelling something drowned out by echoing booms.

BA-BAANNG!

Doors flashed past and Bret dared to look back to see that the cop was getting closer. Handcuffs glinting on his belt, badge shining gold before darkness closed in again to blind them for a few seconds.

The world took a breath and then *BOOOOOOMMMMMMM!* The last firework exploded over the alley, much bigger than all the others. Light upon light, tendrils of gold. The burst swelled, hung, fell, and died out as golden embers in the black night.

In the sudden darkness Bret didn't breathe but stepped instead sideways through the arched doorway of a high stone building. The door was heavy and closed softly.

He found himself standing in a round chamber, encircled by cool, white pillars. The domed ceiling embraced a glass skylight through which a starfield lay and Mars burned red with baleful glow.

Carved white heads sat on plinths, spaced evenly around the roundness of the room. Stone eyes drifted across Bret's face as he looked for another door. Trying to get back home, to bring back news of the mission abort and finish his shots quota.

A green sign glowed EXIT at the end of a dim east-west axis. Bret moved quickly toward it, dark offices and class-rooms flashing past. Under the sign he halted at a thick door with a giant paddle marked FIRE EXIT ONLY instead of a handle. He readied to slam it.

"You'll set the alarm off," said a quiet nasal voice.

Bret spun and saw a single yellow light glowing in an office where a balding man sat at his desk.

Bret panicked, bounced on the balls of his feet, and readied again to plow through the door and sprint.

"A vial will explode and spray you with a bright chemi-cal," the man remarked. "The chemical won't wash off for two weeks. Unmistakable."

Bret stood trapped under the green EXIT glow, mouth open a little.

"Come in here, please," said the man, waving to him.

Bret walked slowly into the office. A faint clicking filled the air. On the man's desk an executive toy stood, a frame from which iron balls hung, swinging back and forth. Tapping metallic punctuality, sharp demarcation of seconds.

"Hey, I'm just moving through," said Bret. "I made a wrong turn, I'm heading back."

The yellow light gleamed dully off the man's scalp, where a few greasy strands of hair lay. He wore square steel-rimmed glasses, also reflecting light. "You've been drinking," he stated.

"Uh," said Bret, "listen, I'm going."

The man gave him a thin smile and looked down at the office phone amid the sheaves of paper on his desk. "You're dressed for jogging, but you've been drinking. There's mud on your shirt. You're in the Philosophy Building, which closed hours ago."

Bret wanted to speak but ended up standing there, bigly, awkwardly.

"You're up to something," said the man. His thin smile puckered farther inward, and he licked his lips. "But it's beside the point. Your rebellion is petty, petty. Petty. You feel that it matters, but it doesn't. You were generated by this system and act exactly as you're supposed to. A cheap product. Boring."

The wan smile returned. The balls swung back and forth, clicking.

"What?" said Bret.

Click click click. The man looked him over and sat up straight, quivering slightly, licking his lips. "Because of your class background, you are a petty owner of capital, and that relationship determines your consciousness. You are alienated because you do not produce. Your world is commodities with prices, nothing more."

Click click click CLICK. The dull patch of light slid around the bald man's head. Bret felt his breathing speed up. "I don't know how you can say that."

"You do nothing new. You were born to be a protector of the current system. Your presence impedes the movement of time: Everything repeats toward exhaustion as negations pile up that will end the culture you represent. I know this." The man steepled his hands and peered at Bret.

Bret's heart raced. He suddenly wanted to take the shiny bald head and crack it on the table. The balls were clicking and clacking, getting louder and louder, sharp gunmetal rounds bursting everywhere.

"If you know so much . . . ," he managed, advancing across the room toward the chair, pulling out his necklace and shoving it in front of the man's face. "What's that mean?" he taunted. "Come on."

The man licked his shiny lips and stared at the medallion. Some time passed, and then he looked up, wan smile triumphant, almost a leer.

"Its signifiers are hierarchical. It's an ideological distraction from the cruelty and injustice of slave-state relations of production."

Bret felt shot, empty inside. He tried to breathe. "That's not what it is at all," he said.

"Of course it is," said the man. "I see right through it. I see right through you."

Bret took a deep breath and felt himself lifting up inside on an aloof column of anger that slid down until it transformed into a small smile. "I have a core you know nothing about," he said.

"No, you don't," said the man, and smiled back, bald head shining greasily through the straggly hairs.

Bret, in anger, thought only of the heights of the eastern hills, of the Punto Nitido Observatory rising above the peaks. *CLICK CLICK CLICK CLICK . . .*

"Those," croaked Bret, pointing at the executive toy.

"Perhaps," said the man, "you will now favor me with a joke about my balls."

"Their Poincaré section holds spatio-temporal chaos," hissed Bret. "The joke's on you."

He whirled around, charged out the door.

The man sat alone in his chair, watching the empty space where Bret had stood.

Bret stood making space in his closet, digging through the pile of junk as he packed for college. He stared at a card he had just unearthed. He didn't know it had existed—the Quick Reference Card for that old computer game Infinity Quest. *He vaguely recalled its manual kicking around at some point, a huge and unhelpful book in like eighteen different languages that kept contradicting itself. Most of it was dedicated to obscure events from the imaginary history of the game world.*

Bret glanced the card over quickly—Moving Your Character, Purchasing Items, *and so on*—but stopped dead when he got to the part about Your Goal:

"Among the thousand objects of the Limitless Dungeon, a single special one has been placed. Your quest is to find it. Once you do, the Dungeon will collapse and you will exit the game successfully. But be careful! The special object is very easy to overlook."

Still pretty useless, but apparently the damn thing was winnable after all. Huh. Bret shrugged and Frisbeed the card across the room toward his garbage can. It plunged right in. Booyah!

Bret plunged into the open darkness of the east-west corridor. A new course had been laid. He traveled eastward now, following like a dream this ghost image of the observatory that burned behind his eyes. A magnetic pull connected something inside him to that distant place of machines. Home was behind him and receding.

He entered the circular room and passed through the center, where the gazes of all the stone heads met and held him for one moment before he quickly broke free.

At the end of the hall he stepped out another door. He sighted the dish—a distant spiderweb against the stars—and moved toward it, following a path lined by spiky plants among the dark buildings. He could make out a very faint bass beat that echoed from the Row far behind him. The house would be totally off the hook by now. His steps slowed until he stopped.

Why the fuck was he going to walk, alone, at night, to the fucking mountaintop *observatory* of all totally random places, and skip out on a massive party at his house and also his twenty-first birthday, which only came once in a lifetime?

The low, insistent beat shifted and it felt like primal fire under his skin. But then he looked up at the lofty wing rising against the stars and he had to shiver.

Despite his desire to get the hell out of where he was, just to move, to *go somewhere,* Bret couldn't. He stood there on the path that was flat and gray and straight, hands clenched, helpless.

Then the policeman emerged wraithlike from behind a building.

"Hey!" he yelled. "Excuse me!" Quickly approaching motionless Bret, pulling out his walkie-talkie.

The path was flat and gray and straight, but as Bret's eyes fell he saw one blemish on its surface. Someone had taken off a manhole cover and a black circle gaped, cut out from the concrete. The hole lay beside a lamppost but the yellow light stopped at ground level, unable to penetrate the inky darkness filling the underworld.

"Hey!" The guard was about ten feet away from him,

thumbing the button on his crackling walkie-talkie.

But Bret still couldn't move until he saw the man's wrinkled eyes fixed on his. Then he jumped into the velvet abyss of the hole and let its warmth devour him.

Bret snuggled deeper into the warm nest of his Captain Planet sheets and pulled up the thick plaid duvet. He coughed. Snow fell outside in gentle drifts, except when occasional blasts of wind drove it against the window right next to his bed.

He sipped ginger ale from a glass and listened to all the voices and the music coming from downstairs. He coughed as he watched Teenage Mutant Ninja Turtles *on TV.*

A woman came and knocked on his door. "Hi, Bret," she said.

"Hi," said Bret.

"Can I come in," she asked.

"Okay," Bret said, and coughed.

The woman was wearing high yellow rain boots and had a knit bag over her shoulder. Cold radiated off her brown coat. "Aw, it must be no fun to have the flu on Christmas," she said.

"Who are you," asked Bret.

The woman blinked. "I'm your aunt Dorothy. And you *are my nephew Bret."*

She was standing right in front of the TV. "Mind if I sit down," she asked.

"Okay," said Bret. She sat down on a chair next to his bed, under his solar system poster, and now he could see the TV again.

"I'm sure your dad or mom mentioned me sometime . . . ," she prompted. "I was there when you were born."

Bret coughed and looked down at his blue and green Captain Planet sheets, and thought. "No," he said.

"Oh. Well." She swallowed. "Well, I have a Christmas present for you," she said, and held up her bag.

"What is it," asked Bret.

She reached into the sack. "I make these, Bret. I'm what's called a potter. Okay, here we go." The woman pulled out something wrapped in newspaper.

"Merry Christmas!" she said, and handed it to him.

"Thank you," said Bret, like he was supposed to, and coughed a lot.

He pulled off the newspaper, which fell in shreds. He uncovered a shiny bowl with dozens of little pictures painted on it: some of sunny days, open fields, stars, others of darkened faces, tall buildings, lightning. The pictures formed an intricate mosaic of color and shape that spelled out his name: BRET.

"It's an everything-bowl," the woman explained. "And it's just yours. You can put whatever you want in that."

A coughing fit suddenly seized him and the bowl slipped out of his fingers and smashed on the wood-plank flooring.

Bret was trying to say "I'm sorry" over and over again at the same time he was coughing. The Teenage Mutant Ninja Turtles were kicking Shredder's butt on the TV.

Then the coughing died and Bret and the woman looked down at the smashed pieces of the bowl on the floor. All the pieces were mixed up, colored fragments overlapping. The heating ducts turned on with a soft whoosh.

Then the woman smiled. "Well," she said. "I think it's much more interesting this way. I can see other things in it now."

So Bret and the woman sat there for a while and found new patterns and designs in the shards of the everything-bowl, and together they told a long story about what they saw. Bret even forgot to cough. Then the woman carefully swept up all the pieces of the bowl onto a sheet of paper from her knit bag and put them in the garbage.

When she left, Bret made a cave out of his Captain Planet sheets and sat alone in that world washed in blue and green.

Much later on he got hungry and went down to find some cereal. The kitchen was big, bright, white, light, cold. The Christmas party was over but Bret could hear his parents' voices through the doors to the big dining room.

His mom: ". . . your possibly schizophrenic sister come nosing around for a handout?"

His dad: "It's incredible what a production you're making out of this. Remember how you wanted me to tell you when you were overreacting."

Bret took the box off the shelf, poured *Cherry Bunches* cereal, and watched the dry bits bounce around a pure white bowl that reflected the overhead track lights.

"I had clients here, Win. Clients. You don't care. No, you were talking to that woman from your office the whole damn time."

A door slammed.

Bret's mom yelling: "I'm really wondering about your judgment, Win, if you think that was okay."

Bret crunched on *Cherry Bunches*.

The doors to the dining room swung open. His mom came in and saw him and her face switched on.

"Hi, honey!" said his mom. "You're up and around!"

"Hi, Mom," said Bret, crunching.

His mom watched him for a little while. Then she said, in a playful voice, "I bet those *Cherry Bunches* got you out of bed."

Bret shrugged. "Maybe," he said.

His mom sat down on the stool next to him and said off-hand: "Why do you think you wanted some *Cherry Bunches* instead of any of those other cereals?"

He shrugged and crunched fiercely.

"Do you think it was the box? That's a pretty flashy red box, huh?"

Bret started to cry. In their bone-white bowl, dried red cherry pieces lay.

○ ○ ○

Red bulbs punctuated the blackness with a cherry glow, like iron cooling from a great heat; the underworld turned out to have its own light.

A lot of frosh descended once to explore the steam tunnels at Poniente. Some of Bret's buddies took the trek but he was away, somewhere on a rugby trip to ASU and Havasu.

He climbed down countless ladders through steam tunnels barely high enough to stand in. His outstretched arms brushed columns of pipes covering the smooth concrete. At irregular intervals those walls would explode outward to cup spacious and forgotten chambers lined with strange machines and rows of molding valves. It would be a tight place to have a rave, he thought.

Bret approached the lower depths. Behind one rusted grill he saw an infinity of perfect blackness. But there, at some fathomless distance and height, a single white light glowed. Distant, impossible light. Nothing could be shining so far down and so far away, away in total darkness.

(Now the Outer Chamber is completely dark. The Brotherhood waits silently. The Candidate is brought in, blindfolded, to stand before Oranos. Oranos is wearing a deep blue robe with silver stars. Even if there are many Candidates for Initiation, the Ritual must be performed individually with each Candidate.)

Oranos (Pledge Educator): I am Oranos, Lord of the Sky. Together with my consort Earth, I was born of Chaos at the foundation of reality, and am the father of all form. You, pilgrim, have passed [number of months] months in a probationary period of pledgeship, where you have suffered many ordeals and learned the meaning of service and devotion to your goal.

Since you have bravely and faithfully persevered and overcome all obstacles that beset you, I will grant your deepest desire. (Pause.) Tell me, pilgrim, what do you truly want?

Candidate: I desire to be initiated into the Mysteries of the Pi Alpha Kappa Fraternity.

Oranos: (Pause.) I see that you speak truly.

(Oranos claps his hands twice. The Warden opens the doors to the Inner Chamber.)

Oranos: You who wish the Mysteries, enter the abyss and bring me forth what is missing. Once inside the Inner Chamber, you may remove your blindfold.

(The Warden pushes the Candidate into the Inner Chamber and closes the door. The Inner Chamber is completely dark, except for a single white candle burning at the point farthest from the door. The Candidate removes his blindfold and finds the candle. He brings it back into the Outer Chamber where the Brotherhood waits. As soon as he sets foot in the room, all the lights are suddenly turned on.)

Brothers (in unison): Hail, Prometheus, bringer of light!

Oranos: These are the Mysteries of the Pi Alpha Kappa Fraternity. The universe is change. The essence of change is the fire that underlies all creation. It consumes old forms and brings forth new. This fire is under the control of man, yet men are also controlled by it.

(The Grand Officer, in his purple robes, rises from his chair.)

Grand Officer: This is the secret truth of our Fraternity: Pyrkagia ananeonei katheti.

Brothers (in unison): Pyrkagia ananeonei katheti.

Grand Officer: From this truth come our initials, Pi Alpha Kappa. In English, these words mean "fire renews everything."

Brothers (in unison): Fire renews everything.

Oranos: I shall soon be killed by my son, Time.

And so on.

Everyone thought that the Ritual was cool. Everyone was supposed to memorize it. Forty percent, plus or minus four, actually had. One hundred percent could fake it really well. No one had any idea what it meant. Bret had a suspicion but was unsure.

Confused about direction, Bret moved back from the grill and wandered off through the labyrinth of tunnels and tubing.

The passages dead-ended in a plain chamber with a

single white lightbulb. A ladder hung down from a shaft rising from the center of the room. Bret couldn't see the top but began to climb anyway.

He climbed for countless time, an eternity of hand-over-hand in tight space of warmth and featureless walls.

The ladder stopped a few feet below a rough stone roof. Bret banged on it: solid rock. No exit. His heart pounded. He breathed thick air in gasps. The ladder trembled and little flakes of stone crumbled from the walls and fell past him and vanished into the endless shaft of blackness beneath his feet.

A brief noise escaped his lips and he swung back from the ladder by his fingertips. He closed his eyes and couldn't tell where he was and where the darkness was. Letting go— was he still holding on?—would just mean a vanishing of nothing into nothing.

Darkness.

Bret's eyes snapped open in the shaft. No, he wasn't Russ Turner material yet. He wasn't going to disappear that easily.

He wrapped his left arm around the ladder rungs and heaved his right upward with all his strength. He pushed and strained and sweated and gritted his teeth and his heart raced.

No movement. A wall of stone.

He braced himself and redoubled his effort until his head was throbbing and his arms were on fire and spots were bursting in his eyes.

Then it looked like maybe the ceiling had slid back a little, and little by little it slid more. An inch, two inches, until it turned out that it wasn't a ceiling at all, only a lid.

Bret got his fingers in the crack and hauled, shoving the heavy wedge back a good foot and a half. Then he pulled himself up and out of the shaft into a gentle breeze.

The night air blew softly around Bret and Caitlin.

"I can't believe you've never wanted to come up here before," said Caitlin.

They were climbing the high eastern hills, stepping through scrub brush and chaparral on a dusty path winding upward.

Bret shrugged. "I never had a reason to."

Nothing sounded except for crickets and the soft rush of a passing car from the street below. As they rose, their surroundings dropped away on all sides and they stood more and more completely within the bowl of star-sprinkled sky.

"It's supposed to be a great view," said Caitlin. "Remember, I'm a tourist."

Bret smiled a little. "All you need is the annoying camera."

They reached a point about halfway up the hill, a flattened outcropping where a fallen log lay under a scraggly tree. "This looks like a good spot," said Caitlin.

"Works for me," said Bret.

They sat down on the log and Bret looked out. Beneath them the buildings of the Poniente campus fell away like toys tossed carelessly around a playroom. The playroom itself was a cage whose pinprick bars were formed by yellow sodium fireflies. Ubermann Needle was a vulgar Rastel Build-ix project; the library, a Gemco puzzle cube. PAK, a peripheral Monopoly house at a far corner of the cage of firefly light, beyond the diamantine grow-it-yourself crystal of the Technology Quad. Past the cage of toys, dark water filigreed by silver moonlight sparkles stretched out to consume the horizon.

"Wow," said Bret.

"It's good to have some perspective, you know?" said Caitlin.

They sat for a while in soft air above the tiny toy school. The breeze carried rich hints of wildflowers.

"You know what this reminds me of," asked Caitlin, after a while.

Bret's heart started to pound. The log was rough and he chipped at the bark with a fingernail.

"What," he asked calmly.

"Like when we all went skiing up at Scott's senior year," she said.

"Really," asked Bret.

"You know," she said. "The great view."

"Oh," said Bret. "Yeah." His mouth felt dry.

"We didn't really talk so much after that," she said.

"Yeah, we did," he said quickly.

She didn't say anything, just ran her foot across the dirt. They listened to crickets.

"I want you to do what you—," she started.

His fingers clenched and gouged out a chunk of wood. "I am!" he said. He tossed the piece at the ground. "Don't worry about me, I'm fine, okay?"

He leaned his head back against the tree and looked up. A great wingspan rising in starry darkness. He swallowed. At the top of this mountainous hill the impossibly large skeleton dish of the Punto Nitido National Observatory erupted. Through its latticework frame a billion stars irradiated.

His eyes dropped back down again.

They sat in silence in the soft air, a distant breath of the ocean.

Then Caitlin spoke in a little voice. She was looking at the ground. "Anyway," she said, "I'm your friend. You can call me if you want to, okay?"

Bret sat staring out at the stars around them and Caitlin bit her lip.

"Bret?" she said finally. He looked back at her, her head tilted gently.

"Are we gonna hook up," he asked.

She faltered. With a tear running down her cheek, she kissed him, a speck on the eastern hills.

15

A dot before the Pacific Ocean, Bret climbed out of a concrete hatch under a violet-black sky spattered with stars streaked through by the Milky Way.

The hatch lay on the beach at the base of the cliffs. As Bret's head rose above dune grass, the ocean became the horizon. The moon was full and bright over the waves, flecking them with sparkling and shimmering silver. The cool breeze blew softly as his feet stepped onto sand.

He felt dizzy and stopped to rest, listening to the quiet slapping of waves. The Row was near the water. He could get back to his house by following the beach to the south, passing beyond the dark cylinders of the freshman dorm towers.

He set off along the shore, uncounted minutes of silent footprints in sand, a small form trudging beside the eternal roll of shimmering waves.

The windswept coast looked empty, but halfway toward the dorm towers moonlight picked out one other distant figure on the sand. Coming toward him. Probably just an aging hippie who slept out here.

Or an officer? Was it an officer? There was nowhere to run.

A few hundred yards from the base of the Towers the figure was right there and Bret saw the white UCONN cap of Darron Moore.

"Bret?" he said.

"What up," said Bret.

"Dude, I got kicked out of your house."

"That sucks," said Bret.

"I've just been like walking around, waiting for my ride. . . ."

"Oh, yeah," said Bret.

Darron looked at him, standing there in sparkling silver light. Bret blinked.

Darron's eyes widened. "Oh, no, you *didn't*. . . ."

Bret shifted a little. "What?"

"Holy fuck, you did!"

"Did what?"

"Oh my God, you are such a fucking asshole."

Darron walked away like a couple of steps. Then he spun around and bellowed in Bret's face at the top of his lungs: "I always stuck up for you!"

Then he turned around and started to go away for real. Bret stood there for a second.

"It just seemed . . . easier . . . ," Bret said softly.

Darron was fading away into the moonlight as Bret repeated, "easier . . ."

But Darron stopped. He turned back to face Bret. "Easier?" he spat. "Easier to throw out the guy who was your best fucking friend for five years?"

He started advancing. "Easier than what? Huh? Easier than *what*? Huh?"

Bret stumbled back and tripped over a little hill of sand and hit the ground in a tangle of windpants.

"I'm sorry," he choked out. Something had gone terribly wrong and this old bit of film had stuck in the projector and derailed the whole movie.

He had no idea what to do. He tried to stand up but none of the angles made sense, so he just closed his eyes and curled up on the warm, damp sand.

"I'm really, really sorry . . . ," he managed to say.

Darron stared at Bret huddled on the beach, a black shape holding itself. "I'm so sorry . . . ," Bret said.

Darron sighed. "Whatever. It's cool."

But it was like something had snapped and Bret kept saying it over and over: "I . . . I'm so sorry. . . ." His shield to stay safe as he waited for this projection-booth crisis to end, for things to get moving again, for the old film to feed away forever.

The breeze picked up, rustling a line of palms, and then died.

After a little while Darron asked, "You're pretty wasted, huh?"

Bret's pleading trailed off. He tried to indicate a number with his fingers. "I drank fourteen," he said. "It's my twenty-first birthday," he added.

"Happy birthday," said Darron.

"Thank you," said Bret.

Waves washed in and waves washed out. The palms rustled and then stopped rustling.

"What happened to you," asked Darron.

"You mean like after junior high?" His voice a little muffled by sand.

"No," said Darron. "I mean like what *happened* to you?"

"Hey, Darron . . ."

"Yeah?"

"What does this mean?" The black shape struggled onto its elbows and something gold shone in the moonlight. Holding it out in his hand.

Darron knelt down and examined the necklace.

"I don't know," he said, after a while. "What?"

"No," said Bret. "I don't know either."

Darron looked at the disc again. Waves splashed against one of Bret's shoes. "I don't know," he said. "Just . . . this is too weird."

Suddenly Bret was standing. "Yeah," he said. "Come on. Let's get you laid."

Darron's mouth hung open.

"I'm not that wasted," Bret explained. "I got a high tolerance. Come on. You know you want play."

He put out a hand and hauled Darron to his feet and put his arm around Darron's shoulders.

Darron looked off into the distance over the sea waves and mumbled with a sad smile, "Boy, is this a brave new world."

Bret nodded toward the two circular buildings looming above them at the top of the cliff stairs. "Those, my friend," said Bret, "are filled with freshpeoples."

Darron grinned and shook his head. "Soon not to be so fresh."

"You know it. Aw, come on." Bret pointed up at the Towers.

The stewardess pointed up. "Did you store anything in the luggage bin," she asked. Bret shook his head.

"A suitcase," said the businessman sitting next to him.

She fiddled with the bin and slammed it and went away.

The businessman had gray nose hair. He was reading The Economist, *pants hiked high above his black socks. Bret glanced over.* AMERICA'S LOST DECADES: SINCE 1979, U.S. REAL WAGE REMAINS STAGNANT.

After a while Bret pulled out the free headphones and

plugged them in. "Seasons change with the scenery, weaving time in a tapestry. . . ."

It was very dry and cold. He shifted under a thin synthetic blanket and pressed his head against the hard humming tan walls. Outside a double plastic window his plane flew in soft roar toward the scarlet horizon where his college waited. Venus burned green over endless miles of rectangular farmland.

Soft chimes sounded and Bret tried to sleep. Later he chose meat over fish, while the businessman bought a tiny bottle of airline whiskey and did a shot. The airplane climbed higher.

Bret and Darron climbed the winding cliff steps to the base of the Kingsfield Towers First-Year Residential Complex. Those two gray cylinders protruded a brutish fifteen stories on opposite ends of a grim concrete courtyard bathed with green-tinged light. Between the Towers lay the low, flat abomination of Dining Services, windows dark. Its big mural of dancing forks and knives and pasta took on a ghastly sheen under the green light.

Music played somewhere, muted by the thick walls of one of the Towers. The courtyard was empty.

"Not so happening," said Darron.

"Hells yeah, it's happening!" Bret said. "Each of these mofos has one thousand frosh. Five hundred froshettes. I lived"—he pointed to one of the greasy windows—"there."

Only a few rooms were lit. "So where is everyone," asked Darron.

Bret cupped his hands and screamed up at a Tower. "Where are you, freshpeoples?" His words became a tinny, ringing echo.

"They're at our party," he concluded, before realizing that was a bad thing to say. He glanced over at Darron; it didn't seem to have registered.

They chose the entranceway to the left Tower, Plexiglas panes gripped in metal frames. The inside door was locked. Behind the Plexiglas they saw an off-green lobby and a bank of elevators.

Bret yanked the door really hard and the Plexiglas shook. Definitely locked. He pressed three random buttons on a heavy copper intercom box sprouting from the dirty green floor.

Lights flashed on the box. Pause. A distorted voice squawked, "—ello?"

"It's John," said Bret.

A pause. The box rasped: "—ait, 's hoo?"

"It's John, man," said Bret.

A pause. Bret mouthed to Darron, "They can't hear us either."

A burst of static from the box.

"Come on, man," said Bret. "It's John."

A pause. The door buzzed open.

Their footsteps clunked across green tile, past walls of

identical metal mailboxes. Bret unstuck his shoes from the gummy rubber floor of the elevator, asking Darron, "What's your lucky number, bro?"

"Um, I guess, nine," said Darron.

Bret laughed. "I hope it's really lucky." He hit the button and it lit up.

The elevator reeked of smoke. When its doors clanged open they stepped out into a common room with stained gray carpet and a couple of sofas.

Three guys on one of the couches had Xbox hooked up to the TV. "Oh! Shoot 'im! Shoot 'im!" one of the guys was saying. Amped-up game music played, lots of high notes racing fast.

At the other side of the common room a fire door opened onto a long hallway with dozens of rooms on both sides. A paper banner hung from the ceiling. Shaky but colorful Magic Marker lettering read HAVING THE NINE OF OUR LIVES! A few sketches of cocktail glasses among patches of glued-on confetti. Colored streamers stuck to the ceiling with thick wads of masking tape. The bottom of the banner had torn where people hit it as they walked through the hallway door.

"Wow," said Darron.

Bret looked at the banner. "Yeah, that's like their theme. Each hall has a theme. We were 'Heav-TEN' over in the other Tower."

Darron walked over and batted a streamer.

"The RAs put up tons of cotton everywhere for Heav-TEN." Bret headed to the sofa, where the three guys sat staring up at the TV, pounding their controllers. ("Oh, Andrew got the ammo pack with the converter!")

"Yo, frosh," said Bret. "Where are the freshwomens?"

"So is it supposed to be 'Having the *Time* of Our Lives' or 'Having the *Night* of Our Lives,'" Darron asked.

"Yeah, that too," Bret added.

A pause. Without turning around, one of the guys answered, "They're in their rooms," in an "obviously" tone of voice.

"Why're you playing video games," asked Bret tightly. "There's *parties* tonight."

A pause. "So," one of the guys asked quietly but clearly.

Bret blinked. "So you should go to parties, you fucking tool."

Whispered conversation among the frosh. They decided to just let it pass and ignore Bret. Bret stared at the one guy's back.

"Dude," Darron said, putting his arm on Bret, trying to move him away.

A girl with long wavy hair walked into the common room from the hallway. She was wearing blue plaid sleep bottoms and a gray T-shirt. She was definitely cute. Not hot, but cute. She grabbed a battered notebook from one of the sofas and started to leave again.

"Hey, what's up," said Bret. The girl turned around.

"I'm Bret and this is my boy, uh, Darron."

"'Sup," said Darron.

The girl smiled a little. "Hi, Bret," she said. "Hi, Darron."

"What's your name," asked Bret.

"Erica," she said. "Nice to meet you." Erica looked toward the hallway.

"Yeah, I'm in PAK," said Bret quickly.

Erica cocked her head. "That's a frat, right," she asked.

"Yeah, it's a fraternity," said Bret.

"Is that a good one?" Slight pause. "I'm sorry, I don't know much about the Greek system."

Darron was giving Bret a look.

"You don't know about the Greek system," Bret repeated, quizzically.

Erica shook her head, hair cascading, and shrugged. "No," she said. "It's just not my thing."

"Oh," said Bret.

She looked at Bret and quickly added, "My roommate's really into it, though. She's pledging one of them. God, it's, um, I can't remember which one. . . ."

"Whatever," said Darron. "Bret here's really into it, though."

"Are you guys both in the same frat," she asked.

"You don't call your country a cunt, you don't call your fraternity a frat," mumbled Bret.

"It's not *my* fraternity," said Erica.

"I actually don't go here," said Darron. "I go to school in Connecticut."

"That's cool!" Erica smiled. "What brings you out West?"

"My sister's at UCLA and some of her friends and me drove up."

"Your sister goes to UCLA?" said Bret.

"Yeah," said Darron.

"Wait, you don't know why your own friend's here," Erica asked.

"No." Bret shrugged. The girl stared at him.

"We didn't have a lot of time to catch up," explained Darron.

"I came this close to going to UCLA," said Erica. "But they didn't want me. Humph." She laughed, pretending to be pissed off, but also a little embarrassed.

"Well . . . ," said Darron. "You know, I don't know. Like my sister's having a good time, but I'm sure you guys are too, here."

Erica swept an arm across the common room. "Have you *seen* this place?" A girl pushed past them with a basket of laundry.

A pipe in the wall from a laundromat behind Bret exhaled hot air tinged with the smell of detergent and lint. Low apartment buildings lined the road, maybe three stories high.

Shantarra shook Bret's arm. He looked down at her. She was pointing across the street at some guys messing around with a freestyle BMX bike in an empty blacktop court.

"Them," she said. She looked at Bret for a second and hurried away, pink backpack bobbing down the cracked sidewalk. Then she was gone around the corner, past a grocery store with heavy bars over a tiny yellowing plastic window. WE ACCEPT WIC/FOOD STAMPS.

Bret crossed the road, squeezing between rows of boxy dented cars with the old California plates. The court was on the corner under a huge graffiti-art painting of people standing around the earth holding hands. The picture had been graffitied over again with random tags.

Bret walked out on the court. Four guys Shantarra's age, one on the bike, three standing around yelling. Holding a paper bag, maybe drinking.

"Hey," said Bret.

The kids looked up at him. The one on the bike circled the group.

"Stay the fuck away from Shantarra Lewis," said Bret. The three guys with the paper bag looked at each other.

"Shantarra?" one of them said, really surprised.

"Yeah, in school," another one said.

"Fuck you," said the kid on the bike, circling closer. He had a shaved head.

"No," said Bret. "Fuck you. Stay away from Shantarra Lewis."

The kid made a tight circle around Bret, going faster and faster. "You ain't telling me what the fuck to do. No one telling me what the fuck to do!"

As the bike zipped past, Bret reached out and grabbed the handlebars. The bike came to a sudden stop. The kid lost his balance and almost fell off but put his feet on the ground.

"And you're not telling Shantarra what the fuck to do," said Bret.

The door to the grocery store across the way banged open and a guy about nineteen years old came out. He was wearing big denim shorts and white sneakers and a sleeveless Kobe jersey to show off his muscles.

He ran across the street, yelling, "What you doing to my brother? What's he doing, Deyshawn?"

"This fool talking all this shit," Deyshawn said. "He's taking my bike!"

The guy stepped out on the court and the younger kids backed up.

He got in Bret's face. They were eye to eye. The guy smelled sweet and he had a goatee—and a gold necklace. Like mine? Bret wondered. Could he figure mine out?

"Get the fuck out of here, motherfucker," the guy said. "I don't want to see your face here."

"I told your brother to stop making fun of a girl at his school," said Bret.

"Yo, Malik, I ain't making fun of her," Deyshawn whined.

But Malik said, "My brother say what he want to who he want."

"Yeah!" said Deyshawn.

Bret hadn't gotten much sleep the night before. He was tired and he had twisted his neck in rugby. It would be so easy to turn around, walk away, go back to the house. But Shantarra's face, the empty sheet of notebook paper. The math not done. Vertigo, endless fall, he'd never sleep again.

"No," said Bret, dogged. "He has to stop."

Malik stared into Bret's eyes for a second and then shoved him.

Bret stumbled back.

Deyshawn laughed. "What, fool, what?!" The other kids were laughing too at Bret standing there.

"Yeah, bitch," said Malik, low and calm, stepping forward.

Then Bret dove for his legs, hitting low like football, wrapping and driving. "The fuck—," cried Malik as they skidded backward across the asphalt. Bret hooked his right knee and hauled, and Malik collapsed back into chain-link fence with a clang and hit his head on the metal pole.

"Oh, you dead," Malik said, and grabbed forward at Bret's neck. Bret raised his right arm to block him but Malik's hand swung around and slammed him in the side of the head.

The world jumped, shot through with pain, and Malik came in low again and hit his ribs but Bret was pushing down on the neck with his left elbow. They grappled, Bret trying to hold him to the ground, Malik straining up, and it was working, he was rising, his hand grabbing at Bret's face, trying to get to his eyes, but Bret wrapped his leg and brought him down again and landed with his knee on Malik's mouth.

It had blood on it as Malik snarled with eyes wide, "I'm gonna fucking kill you," and pulled out a knife. Sharp glint, an edge with a flash of light that snaked up at Bret as he pulled back. The hand rose up, and Bret grabbed the arm and tried to bend his wrist backward as Malik turned the fingers around to slit the knife into the back of Bret's hand.

Blood and pain and Malik almost pulled away, but Bret dug his thumbs into Malik's wrist and pushed, driving nail into vein and tendon and the fingers tensed and Malik dropped the knife. His eyes followed it down and he reached and then Bret punched him in the face.

Malik put up his hands and Bret stood quickly and kicked him and kicked him again before he could do anything, and kept on kicking him over and over and over again. Malik just lay there by the fence, and Bret felt derailed because he just kept kicking and kicking.

After a while he picked up the knife and knelt down. Blood spilled out of Malik's nose and mouth and forehead and cheek and above an eye. Bret held the blade horizontal, point against his neck.

He looked around.

"Nobody fucks with Shantarra, okay?" said Bret.

Deyshawn's mouth hung open, and the other kids were frozen in fear.

Bret pressed the point against Malik's neck, and Malik bit his lip and another small trickle of blood flowed down. Deyshawn gasped.

"Okay?" said Bret, nodding. The kids nodded dumbly.

He turned back to Malik. "You wanted to kill me, huh," he asked.

The guy didn't say anything. "Huh," asked Bret sharply.

"I was . . . just playing," murmured Malik through lips broken and bleeding.

"No, you wanted to kill me," Bret said.

He leaned over and whispered in Malik's ear, "But I think you're too late."

Then he stood and turned toward the kids with the knife. They screamed and Bret hurled it down through a hole in the fence and it stuck, quivering, in the patchy grass.

Straggly grass around the concrete courtyard, the huge observatory wing rising up from distant heights. Bret sat on Erica's bed and stared out her window. He shivered and lowered his eyes.

Erica and Darron were sitting on the floor; they had been talking for a while. "I want to get my diploma and get the hell out of here," Erica was saying to Darron.

Bret turned back to the window again and found his old

room across the way in the gray bulk of the other Tower. Light like from a TV flickered inside. Behind the Tower to the right lay the row of palms and the beach and the water rippling in moonlight.

Superimposed on everything, his own faint reflection in the glass. "I'm gonna take off this stuff," he announced to the room.

Erica looked around suspiciously and Darron laughed. "I got clothes on underneath," Bret explained, pulling down his windpants to show jeans.

"Do what you like," said Erica.

Bret hopped off the bed and pulled off the windpants and the black hoodie. As he got the sweatshirt up over his head, his shirt caught on it and went too.

"Do you work out," asked Erica.

"Yeah, I do," said Bret. Then he realized she was kind of making fun of him, a little.

"Bret wants to know what that thing means," said Darron, pointing to the golden necklace that hung shining above his pecs.

"Do you know," Bret asked her, kneeling down.

Erica looked at it, then turned it over and looked at the other side. "Where did you get this," she asked.

"From this woman," Bret said.

"It's pretty," said Erica. She examined it more. "I think it's Mayan."

"No, I don't think so," said Bret firmly.

"Whoa, I'm just guessing," said Erica, letting go of it. "It looks Mayan to me."

Bret stood up and put on his shirt. Erica and Darron went back to talking.

Bret tossed the pile of his stuff on Erica's bed and then sat down and looked at her wall, where she had taped a collage of photos on construction paper. Four girls wearing prom dresses, with guys at a restaurant, at Disneyland, at a game with their faces painted blue: "Kelly, EriKa (hee, hee!), Su-Lin, Rachel—BFF AEAEAEAEAEAEAE . . . !!!"

"What's 'BFF AEAEAE,'" asked Bret.

Erica looked up. "You've never heard of BFF AE?"

Bret shook his head.

"Best Friends Forever And Ever," said Erica. She pushed back her hair and kept talking to Darron.

Bret looked out the window again at the light flickering in his old room. Erica and Darron laughed about something a couple of times.

He passed out for a while. When he woke up again, Erica was leaning her head on Darron's shoulder.

"Hey, do you know what time it is," he asked.

"Late. I don't know. The clock died."

It had. The display was a dark plastic rectangle.

"Do you have any alcohol," Bret asked. "It's my birthday and I'm supposed to do shots."

"Oh, happy birthday," said Erica. "I think my roommate has something."

Bret got off the bed and walked over to the other side of the room, where pictures of Pacific Outfitters guys torn from magazines covered the wall. He found a handle of okay vodka on a wooden shelf next to a couple of Poniente shot glasses.

Bret said "whoo-hoo" quietly and downed the shot.

He looked back at Erica and Darron. He said, "I'm going to the bathroom."

"Down the hall to the left," said Erica.

Flyers tangled on the tiled wall over the urinals. As Bret pissed, he stared at a couple stuck right in front of his face: PONIENTE ACTION AGAINST HUNGER. JOIN THE TAIKO CLUB! What the hell was a Taiko Club?

Suddenly Bret felt really nauseous. He slammed open a stall door and stood over the toilet and puked. He flushed and rinsed his mouth out with water and wintergreen mouthwash from a bottle some guy had left on the counter. Boot and rally.

The bathroom door flapped shut and he stepped out into the hall again. Through one open doorway Bret saw two guys sitting at computers, backs to each other, typing away. Bret watched them for a little while and they didn't notice him. Then one said to the other, "I sent you an IM." Eyes still fixed on the screen.

When Bret got back to Erica's room, he found the door locked; no surprise there.

He examined the two stapled-on pieces of paper where

the words "Having the NINE of Our Lives" danced among little cocktail glasses and confetti along with the names "Erica Cohen" and "Amanda Warren." Under "Amanda Warren" had been slapped a big green cutout ivy leaf that said: "We Love You Amanda! The Alpha Phis."

Yeah, no more second-rate random roommates when there were actual Alpha Phis at his party. He kicked the door once, yelled "Fuck her hard, Darron!" and took off down the hall.

As he plowed through the door into the common room, he held one hand up above his head and it caught the banner and the banner came ripping down.

"Hey, that's our sign!" protested one of the guys playing video games.

"Your sign blew," said Bret. He pressed the button and the elevator doors opened and he peaced out as they slammed shut.

The door rocketed toward Bret's face, but he stuck out his sneaker and the brown wood frame rebounded.

"Look, it's a tradition," he tried.

"So was slavery," called Emma from around the doorframe.

"It's been going on since 1948," he said.

"All bad things must come to an end," said Emma. She heaved on the door and Bret wondered if his toes were breaking.

"Why do you care about a party," said Bret, "that nei-
ther you or anyone else you know actually goes to?"

"Um, it's blatantly racist, maybe?" said Emma.

"That's your opinion," protested Bret.

"Well, MEChA clearly thinks so, and that's why they're
helping out with the articles and the rally and the petition
to the dean."

"Bullshit," said Bret. "You brought the whole thing
up."

Suddenly she swung the door open. The brass number
4 had broken off some so it said her apartment was 1.

Pale little Emma looked Bret up and down, her hair
pulled back into a tight knot. He wiggled his toes. "Why are
you here?" she demanded.

"I'm the Assistant Social Chair," he said, "and the guys
wanted me to come and talk with you because we're in the
same class—you know, like sophomores and stuff."

Her hallway was small and dark and smelled like paint.
The black rubber on the stairs was peeling up and some of
the red floor tiles were missing.

"So you're like a messenger," said Emma.

"Yeah," said Bret. "Sorta."

"Okay, Bret, I'm going to tell you what my deal is, and
you can tell your frat brothers, and then everyone will know
why I'm getting your party canceled, and will keep on get-
ting your parties canceled."

She looked up at him defiantly. Behind her he saw a

messy little room with a sink in the wall, an electric kettle on top of a mini refrigerator.

"Someone in your house assaulted my friend Jessica Keating at your party last year and nobody did anything about it. It's unresolved, it's unjust, and you need to be held accountable. All right?"

"What?" said Bret. "If she had such a problem she would do something about it."

"No, she wouldn't," said Emma, "because she doesn't go to school here anymore because she left. She didn't want to press charges or make things any more public than they already were."

"Then that's what she wants," said Bret.

"No, it's not what she wants," said Emma. "It's humiliation and fear. Everyone's afraid, like the school's afraid this place'll look worse than it already does. Didn't any of you wonder why the police never came during your little Watts riot last year?"

"Look," said Bret. "Whatever this Jessica thing was, it happened a year ago, and it has nothing to do with you and nothing to do with our party theme."

He saw a big stack of yellow flyers on Emma's desk. He made out the word "Protest" written in stencil font.

A quick shudder passed through Emma. "It made me sick to see her treated that way. You don't know what happened. She didn't want anyone to know what happened."

"This is too weird," Bret said. "It has nothing to do with

our party. Why would anybody spend their whole life trying to fuck with us?"

"She was my friend."

Bret squinted. "You guys didn't even hang out that much, did you?"

"We were on the same hall in Right Tower," said Emma.

"No, but like she would always go to parties and stuff. She hung out with like totally different people."

"We were friends," repeated Emma.

"I don't know," said Bret. "Maybe you really liked her, like, more than a friend, you know?"

Emma drew a sharp breath. "I don't see why anything you're saying has anything to do with the fact that your house assaulted a freshman girl and has a racist party theme," she hissed.

Bret's foot was away and the door really slammed. A chip of paint fell off the frame. He staggered back.

16

The elevator lurched to a stop at L. The metal doors rolled open to reveal three guys waiting to go up. One of them wore a blue shirt that read "FIJI Island Party: Who's got the biggest coconuts?!"

Bret blinked and froze. One of the guys said, "That guy's a PAK."

He couldn't take all of them, no way, not on unit fifteen. He blinked again.

But no one touched him. A guy with blond spiky hair said, matter-of-factly, "Your charter's gone."

"What," asked Bret.

"When this gets to GJP on Monday, you're losing your charter."

"What are you talking about," asked Bret. The Greek Judicial Panel was chaired by the dean himself.

One of the other guys suddenly roared: "What the fuck is this bullshit? Are they really going to pull that?" His chest heaved and his hands had twisted into claws.

"No," said Bret, genuinely confused. "I really don't know what you're talking about."

The guy with blond spiky hair put his hand on the heaving guy's shoulder. "Your house almost killed one of our pledges tonight. He's in the ICU and they said he's in critical condition."

Silence. "So what are you guys doing here," asked Bret because he couldn't think of anything else to say.

"We're getting some of his stuff," said the third guy.

"I—," said Bret, and then stopped and looked at them.

The blond-spiky-hair guy said, "Anyway, on Monday, you're not gonna be a PAK chapter anymore. You heard it here first."

"Oh," said Bret. He suddenly remembered that he had left his hoodie and windpants upstairs.

"I'd kill you right now," the blond-spiky-hair guy continued conversationally, "but I'm gonna let Judicial Panel fuck your house even more."

Silence. Bret realized the guy was actually trembling with rage.

"Okay," he said, carefully. "Later."

Bret walked through the group and felt everyone's eyes locked on him as he crossed the green tile floor. Then he swung open the two sets of Plexiglas doors and burst out to gasp the night air, fresh and motionless.

The house felt still, cool and dark. Bret had come in the side door. Elvis chilled by the foosball table in his blue shoes. PIMPS & HOS CLEANUP *read a big sheet of brown butcher paper hanging from one piece of tape. Bret saw his name three lines down. He felt sick to his stomach and just wanted to get this over with.*

A-Rod passed him in the hall, wearing just board shorts. "Stanton, what up," he said, and they did the snap.

"Do you know where Masters is," asked Bret.

A-Rod shrugged. "Check the lounge. Did you get the thing that rugby's at three?"

"Yeah," said Bret.

Bright sunlight burned through the glass doors on the far wall of the huge room. A bunch of actives were sprawled on couches around the TV. A few boxes of pizza with only a couple of slices left lay on the table next to a half-empty case of beer.

Onscreen a crowd roared. Medium angle on shirtless fans painted green holding up one finger and screaming at the camera. Angle on the Poniente Punisher jumping in his plastic plate mail, swinging his sword, making the crowd yell.

"—Punishers leading Cal Poly six to two," a voice was saying. "We'll be right back."

"Do any of you guys know where Masters is," asked Bret.

"I think he's outside," said Tom Hunter.

"Did you touch the Source, pledge?" demanded Frederickson.

Bret half-smiled and headed for the glass doors.

"I think you touched the Source," said Frederickson.

"If you touched the Source, you're fucking out of here," Hollingsworth called after him.

Right now, Bret really didn't care.

He slid the door open and walked outside. It was bright and hot, and he put on his sunglasses. Masters was sitting at one of the picnic tables with his shirt off, tanning and underlining a textbook.

"Hey," said Bret. He couldn't believe he was actually doing this.

"What's up, Bret," said Masters, looking up.

Bret sat down at the table. "Hard at work, huh," he asked.

"I've got a fucking midterm on Monday," said Masters. "Ohhh." He closed the book and rolled his head in circles and cracked his neck. The cover gleamed in the sun: Childhood and Society.

Bret was trying to control his breathing. "Masters . . . ," he started. And then the feeling that had carried him there just went away, dissipated. He was sitting at a wooden table painted red. The end of the bench had broken off into a spike of splinters.

"What," asked Masters.

But Bret didn't say anything. The paint on the wood had cracked and the pattern of cracks had other cracks inside that repeated the pattern.

"Dude, what," asked Masters.

The birds singing in the trees chirped in a kind of rhythm. A few notes, then a rest, then the same notes with a tiny change. If Bret paid attention, he realized he could call exactly when a bird was about to sing and what the change would be.

"Dude, what," asked Masters again. "I'm your big bro. You can say anything."

So most of Bret surrendered and just dropped away inside and let some other voice say: "I'm not sure if I want to finish pledging this year."

Masters stared at him. "Dude," he said, "it's almost over. They're really like not that hard on you. It's pretty easy."

"No," said Bret. "I mean, I'm not being like a pussy or whatever. I don't give a shit about hazing or whatever. I mean, I just don't know if it's really what I want to do right now, you know? I mean . . ."

Masters was looking at him blankly.

Bret completely disconnected from the part that was talking. "I mean, like I don't really know what I want to do. Like I just woke up this morning and I realized there's all this stuff here and I haven't tried a lot of it, you know, and

*I thought maybe I should take some time to like try stuff
and it might be kinda hard here, or I mean, not like that,
but you know what I mean. . . ."*

Blank, blank look from Masters. This part just ran on
and on: *"I mean, I'm not sure really what I'm doing all the
time, I mean like what I really want to be doing, you know,
because I'm kinda not sure maybe like even who I really am,
sort of? I don't know, I'm really confused, I guess, kinda."*

And then he stopped. There was nothing more to say.
He was empty, exhausted.

He dared himself to look at Masters, and did, slowly.

Totally blank look, except maybe a little shocked.

"Never mind," said Bret. His cheeks burned in the hot
sun. He felt a wrenching in his stomach. He wanted to
rewind time so he had never said anything.

The house dog came trotting over with a clicking of toe-
nails on concrete. It had an old green tennis ball in its
mouth. It pressed its cold nose against Bret's leg and he ran
a hand along its glossy black fur but he barely felt anything.
Numbness.

A long pause as Masters stared at him. Then Masters
started talking, slow at first, then getting faster. "Well, like
first off," he said, "let's say you depledged. What would you
do next year? Where would you live? Who would your friends
be? Would you want to live with your roommate again?"

Bret didn't know what he'd do next year. He'd live off
campus somewhere with God knows who. His friends were

*guys in the fraternity, his pledge class, and girls from sorori-
ties who wouldn't talk to damaged goods who depledged.
His roommate hated him.*

"I don't know . . . ," said Bret.

"I mean, would you really want to go out there alone,"
asked Masters.

Pain. "No . . . ," said Bret.

"Second off, what the fuck is 'Who am I?' I mean, that's
kinda dumb, you know? You're Bret Stanton from
Massachusetts. Dayton. No, my bad, Dayfield, right? And
now you're a PAK and you're gonna be activated in a couple
weeks. You got invited to the Tri-Sorority Pledge Semi. You
play rugby. You played football and baseball in high school.
You're gonna be a business major. That's who you are."

He looked at Bret more closely. "You remember how
when you started Rush there were like two hundred guys
here?"

Bret nodded.

"And you remember how we got the numbers down till
we only had twenty? And you told me some of the guys in
Towers who didn't get bids were actually fucking crying and
a couple guys actually left school? And now a lot of them
can't look at you because they're ashamed? Well, Bret, you
were one of the twenty we picked. That's who you are,
man."

*Bret nodded. A black SUV rolled out of the parking lot
behind them.*

"You know what the rest of the campus is doing? Those are the ninety percent of jackasses who didn't get bids," said Masters. "I think if you're confused, it's that chick from your high school who's telling you shit."

Bret let the words flood him, overwhelm him, sink him.

"I mean, what's her game here? Why's she fucking around with you when she's like two thousand miles away? Who is she, anyway?"

Bret swallowed. A plane was flying by low overhead. "Just this random girl," he mumbled.

"Yeah," said Masters. "I thought so. So like if her or you or anyone else wants to know who you are, just remember all the shit I just told you. And you can be even more when you're an active. Maybe Social Chair? Pledge Educator?"

Right, right, if anyone asked who he was, he could just hold up all those things and he was safe. He crushed Patty Cowell's card in his pocket. He didn't need to change anything.

Pause. "I know you're good," said Masters. "I know you're with us." He studied Bret. "I know you'll do the right thing."

Bret nodded hard. He would, he definitely would. How could he have gotten so off track? Inside the house the guys watching TV all suddenly yelled and screamed, "Whoo-hoo!"

"Yeah, I knew you weren't really serious," said Masters. "So I'm not going to like tell anyone about this, because *they might like trip out and depledge you or something."*

"Thank you," said Bret softly.

A long pause. "I'm going to tell you something, Bret, because I trust you, and I know you trust me." Masters looked around and swallowed. Bret leaned forward to hear, brow wrinkled.

Masters lowered his voice a bit. "There is no Source, Bret. It's just a way to fuck with pledges before they get activated."

Bret smiled. The dog dropped the ball at his feet and waited, panting.

"But it's a good tradition, you know," Masters said. "PAK has tradition that makes us who we are. I love that shit. I think I'm going to run for Vice President, Bret."

Bret threw the ball hard and the dog raced off around the side of the house.

"Tell you what, Bret," said Masters. "I think I can get you in as Assistant Social for next year."

"Wow," said Bret.

"But can you help me a little," asked Masters.

"How," asked Bret.

"I think a lot of your pledge class looks up to you," said Masters.

"For reals," asked Bret.

"Yeah," said Masters. "For reals." He tapped the cover of his book with his pen. "You know I'd be a good V.P., right?"

"Oh, yeah," said Bret.

"So why don't you just tell them that? Like talk it up a little, you know?"

"Okay," said Bret.

"Cool," said Masters.

They did the snap.

As Bret left he looked back to see Masters flip open his book and begin highlighting again, leaning on the crooked table.

Uneven concrete slabs sloping under his feet, Bret moved across the courtyard in burning green light. Behind the dirty gray cylinder of the right Tower, just passing through.

Lose a charter now, lose a charter then, what was the difference? No difference—just a matter of time. Bret had seen a house go every year he'd been at Poniente.

Pressure groups, concerned groups, institutional image makeover, hysterical media reports, legal action, protesters, cultural changes, preprofessionalism. Charters yanked left and right; no one fighting back, resigned. Only the most diehard chapters in the Deep South still organized choirs to sing the old songs in four-part harmony. Yeah, *Newsweek,* we're moving with the times. Yeah.

But Bret *was* in motion, passing behind the brute bulk of the Tower.

Behind the Tower the lights cut down as if Frederickson

had come back from real estate brokerage and smashed them all. The sky sealed everything in, black like lead.

Yeah, Bret was in motion.

So where the hell was he going?

"We're going to the left*!" said Miss Cindy, taking a big slow step to the left.*

Bret and the whole circle took a big step to the left.

"We're going to the right*!" said Miss Cindy, bringing up her foot and putting it down to the right. Pink sweater.*

Bret took a big step to the right and the circle turned.

Miss Cindy touched her fingertips together and held her hands over her head. "We're going in the day*!" she said in a high voice.*

Bret put his hands together and pushed them up big and high and tall. Everyone's hands were up high and tall and they laughed.

Miss Cindy brought her hands around until they were down low. "And we're going in the night*," she said in a deep voice.*

Bret put his hands way down low. Soft blue mats on the ground.

Miss Cindy shaded her eyes with her hand, turning slowly from side to side like she was looking for something. "But however far *we go . . . ," she said.*

Bret put his hand over his eyes and turned back and forth to pretend he was looking for something. Everyone was giggling because it was funny when they saw one another.

Miss Cindy wrapped her arms around herself in a big hug. "Everything's all right!"

Bret hugged himself and everyone hugged themselves, grinning. Then he fell back on the soft blue mats and laughed. Later they played follow the leader.

Bret followed the very few lampposts that broke the gloom, feeble yellow glows keeping him on the path probably back to his house. He walked in darkness until the five-story black cube of Levendecker Memorial Library loomed out of the void, its obsidian walls transfixed by white beams from hidden spotlights.

As Bret approached the library, some master control somewhere flipped over and sent water coursing to dozens of hidden jets with a surround-sound rush. Landscaped on desert terrain, Poniente required sprinklers to survive. So in the black beyond the lights rose smells of new rains and fresh earth: Spring in So Cal happened only at night.

Bret fell to his knees. Where the flawless concrete gave way to wet grass, he knelt and pressed his hands into the damp blades and dug his fingers into the soil and bent over to feel the leaves tickle his face and smell their freshness. For a few moments, he lived a world that was only chlorophyll and green and wet.

Then a high nasal laugh rang out and feet came

stomping along the path. A voice was saying quickly, "*Akira*'s so overrated. Everyone I know who's really into anime thinks *Ghost in the Shell* is better."

Bret pulled himself back from the grass. Kneeling on concrete, he saw three guys lurch toward him through the light of the next lamppost.

"Yeah, but they cut so much from the manga."

"Well . . . ," the first guy said.

"It's supposed to be like twelve books, and Motoko Kusanagi has an orgy!" the other voice insisted. "Worlds Beyond has the whole set."

Big backpacks. When they got near Bret, they slowed down.

One squinted at him and snickered. Recognition. "Hey, there, Mr. Cool," he said.

"Hi," said Bret.

But they didn't keep going. They lingered, two pairs of glasses glinting down at Bret who was kneeling on the ground. Bret looked back up at them.

"What're you doing down there," one ventured. The others chuckled.

The faces shifted positions, circled by a yellow lamp-light halo.

"I—," said Bret, and then he stopped and shrugged.

"Is being on the ground the cool thing to do," one asked, and they all snickered again.

"Is your whole frat gonna do it," another asked.

"But if *we* did it, they'd stop, because then it wouldn't be cool anymore."

"Yeah."

"They'd all have to like climb trees." Giggles and snickers and chuckles. Glinting glasses.

Pause. "Hello? Drunk guy?" One of them waved his hand in front of Bret's face but not too close.

Pause. "Where are you going," asked Bret, distantly. It was so late it was almost morning.

"Why, you want to come along," one asked. Snickers.

Suddenly Bret looked him in the eyes. "Where," he asked, his voice strong and clear now.

The guy was surprised into answering. "The optical lithography lab."

Sprinklers hissed in the distance.

Bret said softly, "I think I know what that is."

"Really," said the same guy, and they all snickered and snickered and snickered.

Bret creased his brow and gazed off into the darkness at some distant spot. They were laughing a lot.

It looked like the darkness was moving, flowing into itself, but the air stood still. Sprinklers whistled and clicked. And Bret said slowly, "Wait, that's like when you, uh, can change a surface with lasers, right?"

The guy blinked. "That's basically it," he said. The other guys exchanged glances.

A slight breeze brought a cloud of fine spray drifting

through the pool of light. Shining droplets clung to the guys' glasses and washed across Bret's face; he closed his eyes to feel the mist. "It's like how you can make chips, right? Like without using gases to etch them."

"Yeah," said the one guy. They all fell quiet.

Then the same guy asked, "How do you know that?"

Bret looked up at them and pointed to the massive shiny cube of the library. "I go there sometimes and I read books."

He stood up shakily. Two guys drew back on instinct.

"My name is Bret," he said.

They examined him nervously from behind specked glasses. He could see himself through those eyes. Big guy, frat guy, gelled hair, Pacific Outfitters shirt: bad signs. But then he seemed to be trying to hunch his frame down to their height. His arms hung loosely. Standing there slumping under the lamp he might just look tired and alone.

The one who'd been doing all the talking made a decision and said, "Hi. I'm Jared." He had silver glasses and a double chin and a patchy little mustache. The other guys shuffled around. "This is Alex and Gohar." They nodded and lifted their hands.

"Hi," said Bret.

"Are you a physics major," Gohar asked.

"No," said Bret. He laughed a little. "I'm a business major."

"Oh," said Gohar.

Silence. "It's my birthday," said Bret, after a while. "I'm twenty-one today."

"Happy birthday," said Jared, and the other two said, "Happy birthday."

"Thanks," said Bret. He rubbed his nose. "I have to do like twenty-one shots."

Their faces were polite but blank.

"Uh," he said, "so are you guys physics majors?"

"They're materials," said Jared. "I'm integrated systems."

Bret scuffed a shoe on the ground and looked at the concrete. "You guys are gonna be scientists, huh," he asked.

Pause. "I guess," said Jared, studying him.

"Wow," said Bret, voice faint.

Jared kinda smiled, but he looked confused. "It's not that great."

Silence. "How did you, uh, get started with that," Bret asked.

Jared and the other guys looked at one another, maybe trying to get consensus. "I don't know, uh, I mean, that was just kinda what I did. I wasn't good at English and social studies and stuff. I think it was like pretty much the same . . ." The other guys nodded.

"And there's a lot of jobs in it. You know?" added Gohar. The other guys were nodding.

Silence. "Yeah," said Bret, in his faraway voice. Jared said, hesitantly, "You could do it too."

Bret smiled and shook his head slowly. "No," he said. "I don't think so." He looked into the darkness. Then he shrugged.

"What do you mean," asked Gohar. "You can just go to classes."

"No," said Bret. "I . . . I couldn't."

"Why?"

Bret looked down. "I just . . . I couldn't do that."

Alex stepped closer to him. "Wait, what year are you," he asked.

"Junior," said Bret.

"You could minor," said Jared, pushing up his glasses.

"You could take an extra year," suggested Gohar.

"You still have time," said Jared.

Bret was quiet. Looking at them.

Pause. Alex swallowed. "Listen," he said. "I'm uh, a student advisor for the department. If you wanted to, uh, I could work with you and help you with stuff."

Bret stared off into the dark. His hands trembled slightly. The earth spun and the planets cycled.

"No," he said at last. "I'm sorry, but . . . no."

He straightened up. "It's too late. Thank you, though."

He looked them in the eyes. "Really," he said. "I really mean it."

They all stood there in the lamplight, this big guy with gelled hair and three other guys clustered around him, light on glasses, dragged down by big backpacks.

Then Bret remembered something. "Wait, please, do you guys know what this is?"

He took out his necklace with those trembling hands, and they all crowded around and examined it and talked about it, tracing the mechanical squiggles with their fingernails.

"It looks like it has writing on it," Jared said. "Like some kind of code. You could probably break it with a good decryption algorithm."

Bret looked at his necklace and said slowly, "That might be it."

The night was silent again. All the sprinklers had died, and everyone just stood around, hands in pockets, avoiding eyes.

Finally Bret sort of shifted. "Bye, I guess. . . ."

"Wait," said Alex. He dug around deep in his backpack and pulled out a little airline bottle of whiskey. "Happy birthday," he said, and gave it to Bret.

In silence he walked off into the night, an outline that drank the little bottle down and tossed it away to be swallowed by the darkness beyond the lamplight. Soon the darkness swallowed him up, too.

Bret swallowed, his drink glass so cold in his hand; only darkness up there, as far as he could see. He stood in the penthouse ballroom, a hall of marble and indirect lighting.

Leaning on a brass stanchion that supplied light, he pressed his face against the great windows. Tuxedoed, black silk-dressed babble behind his back.

Pools of reflected brightness haloed in the glass, above the laser-bright night cityscape. He strained to see if arcs were falling from the sky. Were meteorites, predicted, showering? Chemical flames burned in his nose and in his brain.

Movement behind; a sweet-smelling, cool touch by his neck. "Bret. Party, honey, come on." It was his mom, who had dragged him along to New York for the week. "I don't want anyone to see you moping by yourself."

"One sec," said Bret, fingers clutched against the glass. His breath fogged the surface and then dissolved.

His mom's reflection spoke again. "C'mon, I'll introduce you to some people who'll be very helpful for whatever you want to do in life." She giggled.

"I'm looking for those comets, Mom."

"The action's all inside, Bret. 'Fallen Star Gazing' is just a good party theme."

"Just an excuse?"

"Linda Pottersfield doesn't need an excuse to have a party. Come on."

She pulled at his sleeve, and his gaze through the window died, and he followed.

"Don't forget your drink, honey," she called back, looking straight ahead. Which he had.

Bret's mom led him through the crowd, pulling him

endlessly toward a distant, more worthwhile group, toward more laughing faces always far across the room. In this ball-room, in the heart of the city in the heart of America in the heart of the world, all individual shining strands of money and power combined in one glowing point.

Yet they were all dying. Little by little, and the plastic surgeons' cuts and collagen, and the teeth whitening and hair dyes, and treadmill sessions and personal trainers could not break the force of time. Inside, they were animal, organic, bags of bones and tubes that degraded into death.

So the lights here, and the gold, and the music—they were, at root, cracked, tarnished, and shrieking: a trick. He had penetrated that shining, high-up ballroom, but all he saw was more of the same. Where was the celestial shower?

Bret wanted to go to the bathroom to do more coke. He broke away from his mom when she was talking to a pub-lisher and a publicist at the same time.

Along one high marble hallway he found a door ajar. He went in and shut and locked it.

A white toilet in the corner. A silver mirror hanging from the ceiling on thin metal wires. A freestanding black basin. Outside he heard the clink of cocktail glasses. Somewhere, a high, piercing laugh and a jangle of earrings. Bret looked around at walls.

17

Bret looked all around and saw nothing but a faint line of lampposts ahead. He walked onward in darkness. The lead cube of the library now lay behind him in its web of light beams. For some time he continued forward. The path curved gently to the left and he curved with it.

Bret counted the lamps because there was nothing else to do. Twenty-eight. Twenty-nine. He remembered he had already seen thirty-four that night, so he had passed a total of sixty-three by now.

Soon after, the air grew brighter, and the path twisted around a cool blank wall of tan concrete to a wide space pricked by lamps, terraced floors above a row of dimmed shop windows set into the front of a squat building. The Copeland Family Student Union. So late in the night the area was deserted. Bret saw just one bike vanishing in the distance with lights and reflectors flashing.

Bret walked past the stores. Closed and locked, except a neon sign in the Taco Bandito window reminding him that all locations were OPEN 24 HOURS. No one inside except a guy at the counter in an orange apron, drumming his fingers on the counter, staring out at nothing.

Then he saw motion out of the corner of his eye. He couldn't turn his head too fast because the world was kinda spinning. His heart thudded a little faster—police!—but he couldn't react fast enough and was still debating whether to run when a figure stepped from the shadows.

"Dude!" It was J.P., big grin, T-shirt off-center under his sweater.

"What up," said Bret. They did the snap.

"You escaped!" said J.P. He was clutching a white bundle. Oh yeah, the banner.

"Yeah, I hid in the bushes," said Bret.

"Me and Jesse ran over to his girlfriend's room at Crane Hall," J.P. was saying.

A man in a plaid shirt and a woman with long hair and a thick ream of papers stood at the door of the copy shop, realizing that it was closed. Late twenties, grad students. They shook the door handle anyway and huddled up in consultation with a lot of gesturing.

"Where's Jesse," Bret asked.

"He's around here somewhere," said J.P. "We figured we'd rally up at the Bandito and then go back to the house."

He ran a hand through his hair. "Oh, yeah, the cops maybe got Marty," he added.

"Dude, that sucks," said Bret.

They shared a moment of silence, looking down. Bret saw that he was standing on a letter and turned to see the rest of them. Spidery chalk writing looped across the front of the building next to a sketch of a bursting thermometer: THE HEAT IS ON!!! DO YOU HAVE WHAT IT TAKES TO BE A FIRST-YEAR ADVISER??

J.P. hefted the bundle. "Dude, I still want to do this, though," he said.

A faint rattling from above made them look up. Paper signs taped to the metal railing of the third-floor terrace quivered in the light breeze. ALTERNATIVE SPRING BREAK! ΣX DERBY DAYS! INTERNATIONAL SCIENCE EXPO!

The big terrace. The right-in-the-middle-of-campus terrace.

"Aw, yeeahhh!" said J.P., grinning. "You down?"

Bret nodded slowly. "Hells yeah," he said. He flashed the *hang loose* sign.

They pounded up the stairs, Bret clutching the handrail, going slower, slightly dizzy.

On the second floor terrace the big windows of the Poniente University Bookstore were dark, glass doors chained shut. Pony sweatshirts and jogging pants and knit beanies hung loosely from mannequin frames.

Up another flight, footsteps echoing, metal railing cool with surprisingly rough edges. Bret took the bend in the stairs a little too fast and almost tripped.

"Oh shit," said J.P., smiling big. "This is going to be *tight*!" He started to unroll the banner across the concrete floor, white cloth bunched and folded.

A breeze was blowing and it smelled like ocean. Bret couldn't see the water even though the view off the terrace was pretty good. Lights downstairs, paths radiating away. The corner of Krasner, some of the massive humanities buildings, a few very tall palms jutting out of Rice Quad, dwarfed by the sleek distant rise of Ubermann Needle, radiant in moonlight.

The banner was unrolled now. Fraying white cords hung off the sides. J.P. looked at the paper signs rustling against the metal terrace bars.

"Let's get these fuckers down," he said, tearing off the sign about spring break helping Haitians. The white paper fluttered two stories through the air and landed facedown on the ground with a gentle tap.

The grad students looked around.

"Fuck you, Sigma Chi." J.P. laughed as he began to tear down the Derby Days sign.

Bret was standing behind the one about a science convention on campus. He grabbed the thin paper and pulled. It tore easily off the masking tape with a drawn-out *rriiiiipppp*, and he let go and the page fluttered down, joining the Sigma Chi sign in the air.

"Oh my *God*," the grad student woman said with disgust as the signs hit the ground and lay in a crumpled heap on gray asphalt. The man was shaking his head, curly black hair thinning around the temples.

The ocean breeze grew stronger. Salt and seaweed, fish. "Sweet!" said J.P., looking over the railing at the white heap. "Let's get this thing up."

They each grabbed an end of the banner and hung it over the railing. Bret realized the words were facing them and he pointed it out, saying, "Nice."

J.P. laughed. "Ah take da short buhs to da speshul skool," he said, scrunching up his face. Bret laughed and they traded places, turning the sign around so the writing faced out.

Bret knotted the fraying cords a few times around the twisted metal bars of the balcony and so did J.P. "Okay, I got it," Bret said, and they stood up. The grad student woman had taken a few steps back and was squinting, trying to read the banner, long hair blowing in the wind.

"We fucking *rule*." J.P. beamed.

"Hells yeah," said Bret, and they did the snap.

J.P. started for the stairs but Bret said, "Wait up, dude, I gotta take a leak." He unzipped his fly and pissed right off the terrace on top of the pile of signs. Distant spattering sound.

"Oh, my *God,*" the grad student woman was saying again, and J.P. was cracking up, and it was actually kinda hard to aim because the ocean breeze had gotten stronger and stronger.

Then they were on the ground again. J.P. glanced up at the banner for like a split second as it flapped in the wind.

Loud thumping noise. Jesse was banging on the window inside the Taco Bandito, a dark silhouette backed by fluorescent light. He pressed himself up against the glass and began to fake hump it.

J.P. turned. "There's the kid," he said, heading for the shop. Bret and the grad student woman spent a moment together looking up at the banner. A little lopsided, sagging in the middle: YOU COULDN'T COME TO OUR PARTY, BUT YOUR GIRLFRIEND CAME TWICE! There it was. Bret tried to make out the cartoon but he still couldn't figure out the drawing, which was a little blurred to begin with and was now in dimness and flapping.

The grad student woman said nothing. The man was looking at her. Bret broke away from the scene and jogged around the heap of wet fallen paper to the Taco Bandito and went in right behind J.P. Very strong wind.

A gust of wind so powerful it tugged the girls' umbrellas and made the smaller kids stagger a little. Bret stood at the curb and watched heavy drops of rain fall from swirling gray clouds and spatter in a puddle of dark water pooled around a bus tire. The trees blazed red and yellow and gold, and wet leaves scattered like living jewels across the grass.

In bright jackets, kids were pouring out the doors of

Mortimer Gardner Middle School, a sea of colors. Some got right on the buses, others waited around: for rides, to hang out. Girls talking in little groups under umbrellas, looking sideways at other groups. Guys with hoods up raced through the puddles, laughing, tossed around a football on the wet grass.

Bret turned from side to side at the curb and felt the weight of his backpack swing behind him. He was waiting for Martina to pick him up.

A group of five girls kept looking at him and giggling. After a while one girl detached herself and went over. Michelle Lindstrom, in a white headband and white coat, under a tan umbrella.

"Excuse me," she said.

Bret turned around.

"We were just wondering," she began brightly, and looked back at the other girls for a second, "do you have any friends?"

The other girls watched him closely.

Bret felt his face getting hot. "Yeah," he said.

"Really," asked Michelle. "Who?"

"Darron," said Bret, hoarsely.

The bus in front of him turned on its engine. Black smoke, the smell of exhaust. Darron's bus had already gone, leaving Bret alone.

"Okay, so you think you have one friend," asked Michelle. Raindrops pelting his face, pattering off her umbrella.

"He is my friend," said Bret.

Michelle smiled. "No, it's just really sweet that you think you have friends."

She hurried back to the other girls and they were all laughing. Raindrops kept falling, heavy. Bret was trying not to cry. But the rain was splashing on his face anyway, so maybe no one would see.

Searing pain exploded in the back of his head and he stumbled forward. A wet football bounced off him across the pavement. It landed in the puddle next to the exhaust pipe, rocking back and forth a little.

Andy Manville came running over in a Nike jacket and baggy jeans.

"Why'd you do that, Bret?" he demanded.

Bret didn't say anything. His head really hurt. He tried to rub it a little.

"You got your big head in the way," Andy said. "You're such a geek."

Bret's eyes were watering. No sign of the car. Why couldn't Martina bother to get there on time?

Andy pointed to the football lying in the puddle. "Pick it up," he said.

Bret didn't say anything. The other guys came over and stood around him, either sneering or just glassy-eyed with dull contempt. It was all so familiar, a scene repeated endlessly since around second grade.

"Pick it up," Andy said again.

"Yo, pick it up, Bret!" Josh Maples said. He was playing with a lighter, shielding it from the rain.

"You're being rude, Bret," said Colin Waxsman.

"Are you so smart you're stupid," Josh asked. "Just pick up the fucking ball."

Bret was doing everything he could to fight back tears. He knew if he said anything he'd start to cry. He figured they'd try to push him in the puddle, so he stayed back and braced himself as he reached down for the ball. Blast of exhaust, dark chemical stench.

Then he felt weight on his back holding him down and heard his backpack unzip. The weight was gone and he spun around. A book fell out of his bag and he saw Josh Maples holding a bunch of papers. His papers.

"Oh, what have you got here, Bret," asked Andy, taking the pages.

Michelle and the girls came over to see what was going on. With a roar, one of the buses pulled away.

Andy passed pages to Colin and Josh and Greg Halton and the girls. They had pencil drawings of cubes and cubes of cubes and cubes of cubes of cubes rotating and stretching. Raindrops fell on the pages, blurring the lines.

Bret's head really hurt. He stared at them passing around his papers, laughing. His worst nightmare. He couldn't believe it was happening.

"Bret's been drawing squares," explained Andy.

"What a freak," said Michelle.

"Wait, give 'em to me," said Josh. He got the whole bundle together and stood under Michelle's umbrella and flicked his lighter a couple times and set the pages on fire.

Everyone was laughing. Josh dropped the burning mess onto the ground and held Michelle's umbrella over it (Michelle shared an umbrella with Stacy Bendetti) and they all watched the bright yellow flames lick around the pages. Bret saw the white sheets dissolve, his careful drawings burning, turning to ashes, and he was sobbing, he couldn't help it. Tears pouring out, flowing down his hot face, mixing with the rain. He was burning inside, so much work lost, months to draw those, days hunched over his desk. . . .

The other kids were looking over and smiling at him because he was a mess and he clearly didn't know what to do—this meant so much to him and see he was crying, wailing really, this freak was totally out of control. The policeman came over.

"Hey, hey," he said, his dark blue poncho billowing in the wind. "No starting fires!"

The crowd slowly dispersed with backward smirks.

The policeman leaned down, poncho crinkling. His voice was patient but a little exasperated, like he had said this a thousand times before. "Just try not to be a target, okay?"

Shuddering with sobs, sniffing, Bret nodded. The policeman walked away. The wind picked up. Suffering, loneliness—nothing was worth so much pain. Through wet eyes Bret stared at the smoldering ashes on the damp concrete, and now he finally understood.

Everyone couldn't possibly be wrong.

This was all his fault. He had done the wrong thing and he was paying for it.

Cold wind drove the rain, washing the ashes toward the gutter. Under his thin windbreaker Bret was shivering. The bus pulled away in roaring and choking clouds of black smoke.

He knew that no matter what he did there'd be more: more cut-downs, shoves, sitting alone in the cafeteria, cruel jokes, gangs of laughing faces, rejection and torment. Burning cheeks of shame, tears of grief, but he had done the wrong thing and that was his punishment.

Right now he was trapped, but next summer they were moving to Dayfield. Bret swore through his tears, watching the water cleanse the curb: after this year, never again.

The distant form of the policeman paced alone through rising mist.

Images formed and re-formed, the hazy paradise in his mother's glossy brochures. Right clothes, right music. Right movies. Right sports. The gym.

Bret turned his face up to the rain, asking the skies to damp down whatever dreadful light burned within him that made people hate him and hurt him and punish him, letting it die down to embers, so even the smallest spark might be extinguished over time. He would become a cool and *perfect thing, a thing of crystal and mirrors. He let the cold drops flood him.*

Coldness flooded Bret's face.

"Where the fuck were you guys," asked Jesse, mouth full of Taco Bueno Combo Meal.

"Dude, we put the banner up," said J.P.

Soft fiesta music played over ceiling speakers. Standardized, mixed, and distributed to 407 franchises in the Southwestern regional focus area by Taco Bandito corporate headquarters in Las Cruces, New Mexico.

"No shit!" said Jesse. "Where?" Little bits of lettuce were falling out of the taco.

"Outside the dean's office," said J.P.

A few orange tables, a few orange chairs. The guy at the counter had an orange apron and bad frosted tips behind a Quiksilver visor. Laminated orange signs announcing the Tacos Especiales hung from the ceiling, spinning next to the air vent.

"Fuck that's rad," said Jesse, crunching.

"The grad students were all like freakin' out and shit," said Bret.

"B. Stanton! You're a free man!" Jesse said.

"I ran like a motherfucker," said Bret. Jesse passed his white paper bag to the hand with the taco so the other one was free for the snap. They did the snap.

Outside the window, growing wind stirred the fallen

paper lying on the ground, dragging it across the asphalt.

"I'm starving," said J.P., leaning on the counter. "Yo, can I get a Taco Especial three," he asked.

A powerful gust of wind sent a brown branch crashing down from one of the low palm trees and raised the sheets of paper, first a little bit, then a lot. At last they lifted off completely and went tumbling into the sky. Bret watched them sail upward on currents, white specks disappearing into starry darkness, following the winds.

"You want something," J.P. asked Bret. "It's your birthday, man."

"Twenty-one!" said Jesse.

"Yeah, I'll get a Taco Excelente," said Bret.

"And a Taco Excelente," said J.P.

The guy in the orange apron pressed a few buttons on his register. "Okay, a Taco Especial number three and a Taco Excelente," he said.

J.P. looked at Bret. "And a Tequila Bandito," he said.

"I'll need to see some ID for that," the guy said. J.P. turned to Bret and Bret pulled out his wallet and flipped open the flap. The guy looked at it and said, "Happy birthday."

He worked a little pump handle behind the counter and filled a Dixie cup with tequila and put it on the metal counter. This was part of the reason for Taco Bandito's enormous success.

"Thanks, man," said Bret. The wind outside was dying down; Bret saw the palms slow their swaying.

J.P. slapped him on the back. "My treat. It's your birthday, bro."

Bret grabbed the Dixie cup and tossed back the shot. Ohhh, that one was painful.

Jesse turned to J.P. "You're not getting to-go?"

"Oh, yeah," said J.P. "To go."

The guy behind the counter said: "It's too late, it's in the system."

The wind had died completely.

J.P. looked sad. "No worries," said Jesse. "They'd just jack it at the house anyway."

J.P. smiled a little. "Bastards."

Bret stood there swallowing, trying not to be sick again. The guy behind the counter squeezed meat out of this big wax-paper tube into a few taco shells and then tossed them in the microwave to heat.

"What number're you on," Jesse asked him.

"Seventeen," said Bret.

"Niiice," said Jesse, and they did the snap again.

Beep. Lettuce and cheese came out of boxes, sour cream out of another tube, and Bret was handed his taco. Lots of horns in the fiesta music. Everyone sat down at an orange table.

Bret bit into his taco. It was warm and salty and Bret felt really dizzy and sick. He swallowed and took another bite.

Jesse and J.P. were trying to remember where Jesse's girlfriend was.

Time went by. "Yo, I'm gonna like pass out," said Bret after a while, dropping his taco onto the orange tray.

"Yeah," asked Jesse.

"Yeah," said Bret. "I'll meet you guys back at the house," he said.

"I'm coming soon," said J.P.

"You can't pass out till you've finished your shots," said Jesse.

"No, I'll do 'em," said Bret.

Snaps all around. The guy behind the counter was resting his chin on his elbows.

"Later," said Jesse.

"Peace," said J.P.

"Late," said Bret.

Then he left again into the night. When the glass door swung shut he couldn't hear fiesta music anymore. The air was very still.

Outside the U Bret looked back once at their lopsided banner, sagging in dim light. The grad students had left.

Then he chose his path and set off again, the squat tan building receding in the distance behind him until he couldn't see it anymore, couldn't see anything but the monotony of flawless concrete pathway and recurring lampposts.

Again he walked for unknown time. He couldn't tell how far he had gone, couldn't really tell if he was drunk or not because there was so little stimulation, nothing going on.

The silence was intense, broken only by his footfalls. He felt close to home. He closed his eyes and thought about home and rest and tomorrow being a brand-new day. He opened his eyes and for a second couldn't tell if they were still closed or not, the world was so empty.

The desk was empty except for a computer, off. Bret looked at it, and Bret's dad looked at Bret.

The cubicle nestled against the wall in the corner of a big room where phones rang and keys clicked. A black rolling chair on a clear plastic mat. An empty metal shelf hung from low partition walls of gray felt.

After a minute a thin man with a weak chin came wandering past holding some folders. "Gary," called Bret's dad, grabbing his shirt. "Gary, I'd like you to meet my son, Bret. Bret, this is Gary Westwood."

The thin man reeled to a stop and stuck out a waxy hand. "Hey, Bret," he said. A puffy fringe of hair, kind of like a blow-dried monk.

Bret shook. "Hi, Mr. Westwood," he said.

"Call me Gary, Bret," the thin man said. "Mr. Westwood's my dad."

"Okay," said Bret. He tried to wipe his hand off a little on his blazer.

"I'm showing Bret where he's going to be working after graduation," Bret's dad said. "I think he's really looking forward to it."

Across the big room, past dozens of cubicles, wisps of cloud turned pink in dying light behind the city skyline. Bret had eaten lunch at a rooftop restaurant, and amid waving flags on distant terraces along Wall Street he had seen about a dozen men in suits and ties shooting up heroin.

"Gonna do a couple years here before B-school, huh?" said Gary, moving away.

"It sure won't hurt for the apps," chuckled Bret's dad.

A soft ringing of phones, a   'cking of keys. The black computer monitor reflected Bret s face, glassy and curved. His future waited over the gray cubicle threshold.

18

Bret's path ended at the threshold of a brushed-chrome arch. He stopped dead and gazed up at it. Tall palm trees swayed on both sides as cool blue light spilled around curving metal beams.

He took a deep breath, swallowed, and passed under.

Transparent glass buildings surrounded the empty plaza of the Technology Quad, suffused in blue light. The light shone up from glass panels that alternated with lustrous black squares to stretch in a checkerboard pattern across the ground.

Recessed neon tubes wrapped the buildings in tiers of blue. Bret looked through one transparent wall and saw glowing liquids coursing through plastic tubes, luminous readouts in oscillation, laser light pulsing along fiberoptic cable. The air smelled tinny, ozonic; this complex machinery built up and discharged great energy.

Although the Tech Quad was right across the street from his house, Bret had never before set foot on its glowing checkerboard, never before peered through its transparent walls.

He walked through fluctuation of light and dark. Halfway across the plaza, the tinny smell was very strong and he heard the beat of the party at his house. Its warm lights burned faintly through the chrome arch at the other end of the Quad.

But then he turned around briefly to look where he had come from and saw there, above and beyond the wells of light and transparent buildings wrapped in blue, the observatory stretching its wing toward starry heaven.

Bret bit his lip and turned back toward his house. He walked steadily forward.

At the far end of the Quad, right across the street from his house, a small shape lingered in front of a freestanding display case.

As he got closer, he made out the big nose and tight hair bun of Emma Haviland.

He tried to pass quietly behind her, but she turned around in the bath of blue light.

"I remember you," she said flatly.

"Why are you staring at my house in the middle of the fucking night," asked Bret.

"Did you know," Emma said, "that you're a construction zone?"

"What," asked Bret.

"Look at the plan," she said. She pointed at the glass, toward a diorama of maps and paper.

Bret walked over and stood next to her and peered into the case.

"Huh?" he said.

Emma looked up at him. Her eyes were fixed, intent. She seemed very calm.

"They're going to make the Tech Quad twice as big, and no one's knocking down the U. Where do you think the space is going to come from?"

Bret felt speaker pulse and looked through the arch, saw his wide yard, saw people, girls in tube tops, entering and leaving his house in packs.

Emma followed his eyes. "Yeah, it has to be the Row. I just noticed it."

"If you're here to watch us get bulldozed," said Bret, "you're gonna be waiting a while."

Emma shrugged. "Maybe not so long. Attempted murder is pretty serious."

"What," asked Bret.

She examined his face intensely. "I'm talking about the Fiji pledge in the ICU."

"How do you know about that?" he whispered.

"I got like a hundred phone calls," said Emma. "And then I came over to talk with the Fijis and work on a police statement."

Bret stopped, paralyzed. Headlines, evening broadcasts, flash of *Newsweek* cameras. This plaza was so wide and he so small, a dot in the middle of a checkerboard of cool blue light wells and lustrous darkness, lost somewhere between pulse and heavens.

"Oh, Jesus . . . ," said Bret. "It wasn't attempted murder."

"I'm sure you'd see it differently," said Emma. "I'm just helping people understand what it really was."

"But that's *not* what it really was," said Bret.

"Well, we can't ask him, so someone needs to step up and explain how serious this is. I'm going to make sure we have a unanimous vote in Judicial Panel on Monday."

The corner of her mouth twitched. It looked like she was trying to fight back a smile. "But really you should be more worried about expulsions and criminal charges and stuff."

"You're sick," said Bret. "You're here to laugh at us."

"And say good-bye."

"'Good riddance,' huh?" Bret said.

Emma shrugged. "I spent a lot of time at that house."

Bret snorted.

"No, really, you don't know," Emma said. "I came here when I was a kid. My mom worked and she'd leave me with Miller, like PAK was a good afterschool program. I was honorary sweetheart in eighth grade. Even if you didn't like it, you'd care if they closed your junior high, right?"

Bret stared at Emma but she was looking across the street.

"If this place matters even a little bit to you," he said after a while, dizzy, "think what it means for us."

The palms rustled. Behind the windows, wireframe graphics spun on ranks of dark workstation screens.

"It's justice for Jessica," breathed Emma. "I thank God I can shut you down."

Bret wanted to laugh and cry and scream at the same time, and all that came out was one uncertain wheeze.

"You don't care what's true," he managed. "Or what's just. You just want your lesbo revenge obsession. Fucking GDI."

Emma stood speechless. Blue light wrapped Bret and faded as he walked away across the Quad.

Then a shriek rang out that bounced off the sharp angles of the glass Tech buildings, fractured, and showered back down.

"Look at me, asshole!"

Bret turned and Emma was standing quivering, hands white-knuckle clenched into fists. "Do you know who liked your house?" she demanded.

Bret didn't say anything.

"Do you know who really loved going there?"

Bret shook his head.

"Jessica did," said Emma.

A pause. "Yeah." Emma swallowed. "She was so happy

to get an invitation to your luau party. It was the highlight of her freshman year. It was the highlight of her life."

She walked over to Bret. She stared him in the eyes and spoke quietly. "And she met this guy. And he was just this really charming, great guy, and he got her a few cups of beer before anyone else."

Her voice drifted serenely. "And so after she got some beers he made her a drink himself, except this one had GHB in it. She slipped into a half-alive half-dead state while he spent the next four or five hours savagely raping and beating her."

Emma's voice was so quiet. She sounded like she was reading from an internal script. "He threw Jessica into a Dumpster," she said. "She was bleeding everywhere, a thousand cuts, face, arms, breasts, body. That's where she woke up, slowly.

"And do you know what Jessica told me," Emma asked pleasantly.

Bret shook his head slow.

"It was the weirdest thing. She said she actually felt like he wanted to kill her but messed up. Like he would get off on her being dead or dying."

Light wind moved the tinny air and it felt like lightning might split the cloudless night.

"Do you know who she was talking about?"

Bret didn't say anything. Words floating somewhere, a world that was almost blank.

"Do you *know who it was,*" she asked again.

Bret shook his head a little.

"It was your House President Sam Masters," she said.

Bret realized with surprise that he could see actual halogen bulbs glowing under the blue frosted glass of the panels.

Racing somewhere, a flurry of pounding footsteps.

"Tac Pac!" hollered a voice.

Emma's face whipped away. Bret crashed to the ground with J.P. on top of him.

"Oh, man, you have no idea how much I totally saved you there, bro," whispered J.P. "You are going to thank me so much tomorrow."

Bret just lay there staring up at the sky. Behind transparent walls the silent light show went on, glowing patterns in constant change.

"Bret," asked J.P. "Talk to me, man."

"We're losing our charter on Monday," said Bret.

J.P.'s head loomed above him, half in blue light, half in shadow. "What?" he said.

Bret told him about the Fiji. J.P. rocked back into a squat. Bret sat up.

"Why didn't you say that before," J.P. asked.

Bret shrugged.

"Holy shit," said J.P. "I mean, holy shit."

Bret said nothing. J.P. looked around desperately.

"Fuck," said J.P. "I've gotta go tell Masters."

He jumped up but Bret still sat unmoving on the glowing grid.

"Come *on*!" said J.P. He put out his hand and hauled Bret to his feet. Bret felt really dizzy and stumbled for balance.

The last thing he saw before they hurried out of the Tech Quad was that tiny plain figure alone in vast space, disgust and sorrow mixed with shadows on her pale face.

Shadows creeping up the wall, elongated, the sun very low in a bloodred sky. Bret looked up from the notebook paper. Shantarra was sitting cross-legged on her bed in a shaft of red light that shone through the streaked window. Pop music playing softly on the dresser radio, like always.

"Hey," said Bret.

Shantarra stopped swinging her keys, blue cord wrapping around her finger.

"This is really good," said Bret. "You got eighteen out of twenty-one." She had said nothing about the kids at school, just started doing her work again.

Shantarra frowned a little. "What'd I get wrong," she asked.

Bret went over and sat next to her on the bed. The thin mattress bent with a squeak. He flipped through the textbook. Warm air blew through the window, the cloying smell of scented oil, spices.

"What's your necklace," Shantarra asked.

Bret looked down. The disc shone bright in the overfull red blaze.

"I don't know," said Bret. "Do you know what it means?"

She took it in her little hands. A thorough inspection: turning it over, looking carefully at both sides.

"No," she said after a while.

A small smile. "But I like it. It makes me feel happy."

Bret wasn't sure he had ever seen her smile before. A fleeting impression, a glimmer of light.

Lights flashed from the PAK house, framed by deepest night and palm tree shadows. Music pounded and dark shapes staggered to and from the door.

Normally campus rules required parties to close at two in the morning. Normally the police would have shown up by now. But the hour had long ago come and gone.

J.P. hurried across the great expanse of damp green lawn. Bret trailed after, colored lights from the house flashing glassily off his eyes.

A pack of freshmen passed, leaving for their dorm tower. Groups of people crowded the porch but the line had disappeared. The tiki torches had either burned out or been stolen.

J.P. and Bret drew near to where the crowds tangled and fed into and out of the door. They pushed through bodies, climbed the stairs.

It was as if the dean, awake in his study from the late night phone calls, knew this was their last party ever before he obliterated their ancient house.

As if he had ordered the police to stand down, just for tonight. A primeval nod of honor beyond the law, like serving the condemned man caviar at his last meal.

Someone leaned heavily on one of the white porch posts and the brittle wood snapped.

Bret did the snap with K-Money as he pushed through the mass of people packed into the common room under spinning lights. The music so, so loud.

A line of girls with green cups thrust past behind him, yelling garbled messages.

J.P. had run off in search of Masters, and Bret made his way through writhing bodies moving, shoving, falling. He was heading toward the barroom.

The mood was manic, electric. Everyone knew things were supposed to have closed long ago. Only the DJ didn't seem to notice he had played so long past his engagement; he touched controls, standing calm in his own light.

The barroom was unbelievably hot, a blast of heat and body sweat and sharp beer tang. The pledges serving seemed far drunker than anyone else. Slipping and sliding, they tried to roll a new keg over to the ice bucket. But even though they had problems standing, they kept the system in place: Bret got his red cup of beer.

He leaned heavily on the wall in the short hallway to the common room, watching the people pass in heat and darkness. Some people knew him and he let his hands do the snap or smiled vaguely and nodded.

Then the impossible happened: The music volume dipped suddenly. Passing bodies froze, stumbled in confusion. The black shadow of the intercom box above Bret's head clicked on.

"All active brothers come to the chapter room for meeting."

Then the music scaled back up again and everyone returned to movement and laughter. You could almost believe nothing had ever happened.

But the command burned in Bret's memory. He levered himself up on the wall and stood straighter. He turned the cup around in his hands. Half his lifetime had gone into that piece of red plastic. He methodically gulped the beer and shook his head to clear it, packed among the bodies in motion.

19

The side room was still crowded. A bunch of girls were dancing on top of the beer pong table. Some guys were cheering. The girls yelled something, but the music was too loud.

When nobody was looking, Bret did the knock on a plain wooden door in the corner. It opened a foot and he slipped into dry old air with a new beer in hand.

He nodded to Bennett, who was Sergeant-at-Arms and Gatekeeper. The chapter room was about half full. Masters and the other officers were sitting at the front in their robes, talking, on a raised platform under the giant metal coat of arms. Bret took his seat under the broken ceiling fan and sipped his beer and waited while other brothers came in, one at a time.

Soon the place was almost full, guys talking in low voices, hunched in groups. *Bang bang bang,* went the gavel.

Everyone stood. "We are brothers gathered together . . ." Masters intoned.

"Searching for the light in darkness," chorused the rest of the room.

Bang. They all sat. A moment of silence.

"Something very serious happened tonight," said Masters. "Brother John."

J.P. stood and saluted him.

Masters did the sign. "Go ahead."

Bret sat and looked at the suns on the blades of the broken fan and the rest of the guys sitting silent as J.P. told everyone about the Fiji pledge. Outside the door the music pounded on and the room echoed with occasional thumps as something hit the wall.

When J.P. finished the room was very quiet again for a moment.

"Risk Management Chair," said Masters. Willens saluted him. Masters made the sign.

"Were there any actives there when this was all going on," Willens asked J.P.

"Yeah," said J.P. "Bret."

The entire room turned and looked at Bret holding his beer. "Yeah," he said.

"Just you," asked Willens.

"Yeah," said Bret.

Silence. The air smelled like dust. J.P. saluted Masters and sat back down.

"Permission to chair, Grand Officer," Willens asked Masters.

Masters nodded absently. He seemed out of his depth, lost and confused up there in his purple robes in the soft light.

"We talk about individual and collective responsibility during pledging," said Willens. "Do you guys remember that?"

Some brothers nodded.

"Okay, basically, if I go out and shoot Deandra Romapella by myself, I'm to blame. It's totally me. I go to jail."

The world was spinning a little, like everything was scrolling upward, and Bret closed his eyes. He really didn't want to drink anymore.

Willens went on: "But if me and Ken get wasted and go shoot her, PAK's to blame too. It's an official chapter activity. Ken and I go to jail and the chapter's over."

Bret heard him sigh. "Unfortunately we had an active and a good chunk of our pledge class around for this incident, and that means it's a chapter problem. So not only can they take our charter, but probably everyone in this room will be charged with—this is kinda off the top of my head—uh, assault and battery, reckless endangerment, and maybe criminally negligent homicide."

Willens's voice sounded strained for a second. "Obviously no one's going to decide to freely take the blame on this one." A pause. Bret kept his eyes tightly shut.

"Yeah?" said Willens.

"Can we get a lawyer," someone asked.

"Yeah," said someone else.

"No," said Willens flatly.

"Why not," asked a voice.

"It costs too much," said Willens.

Bret opened his eyes.

"What about the alumni," asked Eric Sheffield.

"Alumni Relations?" somebody called.

Willens looked around the room. "Where's Stan," he asked. Low voices, people turning. "Okay, not here."

Bret saw Vice President Tolski write something on a piece of paper.

"Wait, we can afford somebody," said Marty. "We pay like five thousand a quarter, three quarters a year, eighty guys . . . That's a lot."

"Most of that goes to room and board," said Willens. "We only have a little extra and we can't spend that."

"Why not," asked Nick Reilly.

"We have a tight budget," said Willens. "Look, just—"

People all started talking. "Not that tight," said Ryan Yeagermeister.

"Fuck, we can't spend any more, okay?" said Willens.

"Why not?" another voice yelled.

"We have some debt."

Masters suddenly stared at him. Willens was looking at the floor. Bret made himself drink more beer.

Voices babbling around the room. "How much debt?" called someone.

Willens looked up. "Over half a million dollars," he answered.

Dead quiet.

Bang! The gavel exploded into silence. "Risk Management Chair," said Masters. He made the sign.

Willens turned, voice pleading: "I figured we had to talk about—"

BANG! "Risk Management Chair," repeated Masters with ice in his words. All eyes tracked back and forth between them.

Willens paused for a second, saluted, and sat.

Dead quiet. Bret forced down his gag reflex and finished the cup. Muffled beat from outside the door.

Masters stood, purple robes shimmering in the dim light. His words sounded almost mixed up. "The party is going to go on. I'm sorry we were all bothered by this meeting. I promise all of you by the rising light of Pi Alpha Kappa that this will be not an issue. This chapter meeting is over. Officers stay behind for officers meeting."

A pause. Nobody moved. Masters looked down and saw the gavel. He picked it up and looked at it. "May PAK follow all who—sorry, may PAK lead all who follow her path into light ever greater."

He brought it down in nine quick strokes that felt like an eternity.

20

Bret took the long way back to his room, down the side hall past all the fading composites and ripped green couches that now had people passed out on them. A photo of little Emma grinned on an old composite: HONORARY SWEETHEART.

Some guy was lying on the floor. Bret stepped over him. In the common room he waded through a mass of crushed colored cups that covered the carpet and crunched underfoot. People dancing on as the world fell apart, and him so tired and so sick.

He felt girls thrusting against him, frantic, desperate, the feeling, but dizziness dragged him downward into its confetti spiral and he just wanted to get to his room. He swallowed a bitter burp.

Small groups of brothers released before him from the

meeting huddled against walls, in corners, talking in quiet voices. Bret saw some people look at him and he nodded back.

He climbed stairs, plowing through bodies. He swung open the door to his double and kicked it shut behind him.

No Jordan anywhere, the silver textbook lay spread like a dying swan on the carpet. The fucking red light on the answering machine was still off. Bret snatched up the receiver and heard no dial tone, only the cotton silence of a dead line.

"God damn it," he said, and knelt on his bed and looked out the window. An impossibly lightening sky of dusky blue where the stars were beginning to fade over the palm trees. And there in the first dim light, he saw wires hang loosely out of the utility box on the telephone pole outside.

So he sat on his old mattress and felt helpless and kinda bored. Too sick to move, he thought instead: back and forward and forward and back, trying to take a total inventory, to recall something he had heard or had seen, the memory of a particular facial expression, the smell of wind at dawn, maybe, something somewhere that would free him, give him a way out of this stalemate.

He thought of his necklace, and studied its patient gleaming disc like he had a thousand times before. Sun rising, sun setting, light tracing the circles of glyphs, playing across machinelike writing. The symbols whirled around him. He sensed a meaning almost there, but it receded as he tried to grasp it, like a shadow or gleam of light, leaving him staring in the end at a hard disc of metal. Nothing.

The first bird of daybreak chirped outside his window and the bright sound triggered memory. There. No, *there*. He touched the unfamiliar lump in his pocket. That high school chick's cell phone. Connection to the world through the ring of linked satellites that obeyed the tiny plastic box. Gratitude and sadness welled up, overwhelmed him, and there in his tiny cluttered double his hand lunged desperately and he yanked the thing out and snapped it open.

Liquid crystal blobs slid around its wrecked display.

But it had worked well enough to ring. So the screen was shot, so what, he could probably still punch in a number and it'd work. Probably.

He could call for help.

Bret ran down the list of numbers he knew: family, guys at the house, mainly. He thought a bit about each one and crossed it off, because there would be nothing new at any of those numbers, nothing to hear.

Oh, no, *wait*. Wait a minute.

He punched in the number with a shaking finger and hoped he remembered it right and hoped he'd typed it right because who could tell with the display busted like that.

He hit the call button and there was silence and then a ring and another ring and another ring and another ring and then a click.

Pause. "Hello?" said a voice.

"Hey, Caitlin?" said Bret.

"Bret," asked the voice. "Is this Bret?"

"Yeah," said Bret.

A groan. "Bret," Caitlin said. "Do you have any idea what time it is here?"

Bret blinked. "No," he said. He thought a little more. "Uh, I don't even know what time it is *here*."

Caitlin yawned. "Well, it's really late. Early. Something."

Bret cradled the phone with both hands. "I'm sorry, Caitlin," he said into it. "Please don't hang up. I'm sorry."

"No, I'm glad to hear from you," said Caitlin. "What's up?"

"Thank you," said Bret. "Thank you."

"Yeah, you're drunk," said Caitlin. "Hey, happy birthday. Are you having fun?"

"Caitlin, you're the only person who knows me," said Bret.

"Bret . . . oh, God. Don't say that," said Caitlin at last.

"Why not," asked Bret.

"That can't be—I mean, uh . . ." She started again. "Do you really think that's true?"

"Yeah," said Bret. "It's totally true."

"Well, uh, wow. Heh. Thank you, I mean. Um." A pause. "So, uh, what's going on," she asked. "I haven't talked to you in a while."

"My chapter's falling apart," said Bret. "We're losing our house and we're all gonna have to go to court. What am I going to do?"

Silence. Bret panicked. "Caitlin? Are you there?"

"Yeah, Bret," she said. "I'm here. I'm just thinking about . . . God . . ."

"Please don't hang up on me," begged Bret.

"I'm not going to hang up on you," said Caitlin.

"Thank you . . . ," said Bret.

Silence.

"Listen," said Caitlin suddenly, her voice charged with excitement, urgency. "This could be it, your chance."

"Huh," asked Bret.

"This could be your chance to do what you want to do," she said. "You see?"

Bret defocused a little. The lights blurred and pooled. "What's that," he asked.

"That's the thing," she said. "Whatever you want."

"Like what," he asked.

"Like *any*thing, Bret," she said. A pause, and her voice became soft. "I . . . I promise, it's such a different world than like when you were little or whatever." Her words almost sounded like static, sound rushing in and out. "It could be huge, like a totally new start for you."

He swallowed. He stared at the heaps of trash on the floor as her distant voice drilled into his ear.

"Like what should I do, though," he asked.

"Just whatever, your own thing, you know?" said Caitlin. "Like don't worry about what anybody else is doing."

"But what kinda thing," asked Bret.

"You know," said Caitlin. "Something you actually care about."

Bret didn't say anything. Caitlin went on, words coming faster: "Like I remember like years ago at the ski house, when you told me all that stuff, and it was like your eyes lit up, and you seemed like a totally, completely different person. That's what really matters to you."

Pause. "I don't know if I could still do anything like that," he said after a while.

"If—" Her voice suddenly cracked and turned into a blurt, and when she spoke again, she sounded completely different. "I'll be here for you, okay," she said slowly, softly. It sounded like she was crying. "I, I just got out of, well, you know, for my eating thing . . ."

"Really?" said Bret. "I—"

Then the phone played a tinny tune and the light behind its smashed display winked out. He held the plastic box in his hand for some time. He pressed a few buttons aimlessly but since the battery had died nothing happened.

He sighed and dropped the little box onto his mattress.

Cool air caressed the back of his neck as birds chirped outside the lightening window. Suddenly very tired, he closed his eyes and leaned his head back against the wall.

"—birthday—knows—really drunk and partying tonight." The hollow voice of Sam Masters speaking into his skull through grimy white paint.

Bret's eyes opened.

He lived directly over the chapter room.

"—not right." Another voice.

"—think—he—probably responsible anyway—" Masters again.

"—not true." Same voice as before. Louder. Willens?

"—reasonable—assume it was just him—" Masters, low and level.

Bret pressed his ear as hard as he could against the wall. It was so hard to hear over the beat.

"Why would he ever agree," asked a different voice.

"Well—if—answer the charges—some reason—," said Masters. "Off the hook—save the chapter."

Someone said something inaudible.

"—you're too weak—agree—," Masters said.

Nothing. Ringing of walls, the pounding beat.

Then Willens. "Not be a part—"

"—your oath—chapter—," said Masters.

"—me sick." Willens.

"All or one," said Masters.

Another voice: "—idea to—"

Then a new song spun in, louder, more vocals, and Bret couldn't hear anything.

o o o

Ears ringing, Bret sat bolt upright in bed.

The medallion pressed solidly into his chest and he felt warm, as if he were filled with shining liquid gold. He would unravel its mysteries yet.

He lunged for the heaps of paper on the floor, sweeping trash aside to discover a cleanish sheet with only half of a footprint on it and the corner crumpled. Desperate fingers closed around an Oxnard Jeep Service pen with the black cap chewed off sticking out from his econ textbook.

On an empty corner of desk he got the pen working and tried to write but couldn't focus at all, things were swirling too much. He willed the world to stop moving, to make his hand and eye steady, but his pupils tracked away and he felt even more dizzy and nauseous, a lost cause of spinning black lines.

Pen and paper clutched in his hand, he hauled himself to his feet, pulled the door open with a thud, and stepped out into the hall. It was deserted, but the party sounds still roared from down the central stairs where colored lights passed on the wall. He banged on the doors around him but they were either locked or swung open loosely to reveal emptiness and windows of growing light—no one home.

The triple was empty too, and as Bret pulled his head back into the hall he saw Masters alone bearing straight toward him with a big smile on his face.

"Bret Stanton! The man of the hour!"

Bret gasped a little and clutched the wall to steady himself.

Masters was right in front of him now. "Dude, such fucking random shit is going down tonight, huh?" He rolled his eyes in exasperation.

"Yeah . . . ," Bret got out.

"Yeah, for reals." Masters put his hand on Bret's shoulder. "No worries, though. No fucking worries, bro! This is your fucking birthday! This is PAK tradition!"

Bret just breathed deeply and steeled every muscle in his body.

"Come on," said Masters. "I heard you're almost there. Let's do a double shot, huh? Let's get you to fucking *twenty-one*!" He beamed and began to pull gently.

But Bret had braced himself. He managed to say, "Just give me five minutes, okay?"

Suddenly Masters was stern, disapproving. "Dude," he said, "this is tradition. Come on, you gotta represent, little bro. Make me proud you're a PAK."

One poised moment of utter stillness. Their eyes met and they stared straight at each other.

Then Bret spoke.

"Five fucking minutes."

He shoved the hand off his shoulder.

Masters stood there blinking in confusion, opened his mouth and closed it again. Hesitant, late, a feeble smile. "Okay, five minutes . . . ," he said weakly, but Bret was already down the hall and pounding down the stairs.

The common room was pure noise and hundreds of bodies in chaos and Bret struggled and fought through heaving forms with the paper and pen clutched in his hands, slipping and crunching on cups. So loud so dark, no one could hear or see in this suffocating cave.

He made it to the short hall to the barroom and forced his way through the unyielding columns streaming forward and back, churning relentlessly around him like an endless harrow.

"The beer's all *foam*!" an abysmal girl with caked-on makeup was shrieking by his ear, and he desperately shoved her aside as he plunged into a space that was lighter and a little quieter.

A few dozen people with colored cups in hand standing around talking or waiting for drinks. Rob was leaning on the wooden bar and talking and joking with the pledges serving under the coat of arms.

"Rob," said Bret. "Rob . . ."

Rob turned and saw Bret and grinned and held out a hand for the snap. "Dude, my fellow prankster!" he said. "Dude, I fucking ran and hid—"

Bret pressed the paper and the pen into Rob's hand.

Rob looked down at it. "Dude, what the fuck?" he said.

"Rob, please," said Bret. "Can you write something down for me?"

"What," asked Rob, still staring at the crumpled sheet. People waiting for beer were watching them.

"Listen, Rob, please write this thing down for me, okay?" said Bret. "It's really, really important, please?"

A pause. "Dude, what the fuck are you talking about," asked Rob, looking around. Conversations had hushed as more people had stopped to enjoy this scene.

"I need you to write this thing down," pleaded Bret. "In case something, like, happens to me I need you to give it to this guy, uh, Jared in physics, okay?"

Rob looked at Bret. Then he laughed and shook his head. "Dude, you are making absolutely no sense right now, bro!"

He turned to the pledges serving. "Hey, get my man here another beer, okay?" He looked back to Bret. "Dude, what number are you on," he asked. "You're almost there, huh?"

"No, listen," said Bret. "Rob, I need you to please write this down."

". . . the Fraternity Man of the Year . . . ," a girl was whispering.

The pledge put a red cup of beer on the bar next to Bret's elbow. "There you go, homey!" said Rob.

"Rob, come on, please, help me!" said Bret. He grabbed Rob's shirt.

"There's gonna be a fight," Bret heard some sophomore saying behind him.

"Whoa there, stallion," said Rob. "We'll like talk about this tomorrow." He was looking around and smiling at people in the crowd that was now quiet and standing around watching them. He lowered his voice. "Dude, you're wigging out, what the fuck did you take," he asked.

Bret looked around desperately, turned to see the bemused eyes of maybe half the room behind him. More people kept filtering in, the beat outside, the heat, the sticky floor.

In the coat of arms painted over the bar, the torch of Prometheus burned on the field of eternity under the lights of the Lord of Heaven. Bret let all of himself fall away except for one small part that reached his hand out to pick up the red cup.

Rob smiled.

Bret turned to the crowd. "This," he said, "is the cup for hot-ass girls we want to get shithoused and sleep with and for cool motherfucking guys who are basically us."

Rob's face froze. All conversations stopped.

Bret dropped the red cup. It hit the floor and beer splashed. "I think there was a mistake," he said. He crushed the plastic under his shoe.

He reached over the counter past the unmoving pledges to where the cups were stacked. His fingers closed around a clear one. "This," he said, and held it up for everyone to see, "is the cup for nerds and freaks. You don't touch it, you don't serve it. It's outside the system."

Light shone through the transparent sides of the empty container. "This is my cup," said Bret.

No one moved. No one spoke. The music seemed to fade away.

Bret turned to Rob. "Please write this down," he said.

Rob picked up the pen in almost a trance.

"This is a formal proof," said Bret, "of how to open Minkowski space-time without using exotic matter. Minkowski. M-I-N-K-O-W-S-K-I. Subtitle: 'Creating Wormholes and Time Warps Through Vacuum Energy Density Fluctuations.'"

Rob's hand moved slowly on the page, copying the words carefully in solid black print.

"Okay," said Bret. "Consider a d-dimensional space M. . . ."

"Um." Bret took a breath and tried to focus better. "A space M." There was a long pause. Bret looked at all the faces watching him silently.

Bret pinched the bridge of his nose. "Sorry," he mumbled. "Uh, one second, sorry . . ." He closed his eyes, but only saw blackness. He couldn't remember anything at all. The liquid gold had evaporated, leaving emptiness at his center. Only a shell was left, wrapped around no core. He didn't know why he didn't just crumple.

Bret opened his eyes again. "Sorry," he said again, in a higher pitch. His heart pounded like ritual drumbeats across the savanna.

His shaking hand dropped the clear cup and it bounced with a soft pop on the hard linoleum.

Noise returned slowly and embarrassed eyes avoided his. The paper drifted forgotten to the floor and soaked up sticky bar tar. Conversations returning, new laughters beginning, hands helping Bret off to the counter along the wall.

"—on something," Rob was saying apologetically.

Jordan was there with a new red cup of beer for him. "Dude, I know," Jordan said. "Birthdays are hard. Remember how on my twenty-first I was like crying? Everyone fucking embarrasses themselves."

Bret was shuddering, shivering. People kept looking over, but it wasn't that interesting, so they looked away again. He glimpsed between shoes the paper dissolving into soggy shreds in the muck.

Jordan pointed to the beer that sat waiting for Bret on the side counter. "You're almost done, right," he asked. "Then you can just get some fucking sleep."

"Can't," croaked Bret.

"Dude, trust me, you'll feel like ass for the next two days," said Jordan, looking around the room. "Fuck, I was gonna tell you something."

"No . . . ," said Bret. "I've gotta. Got to—"

"Oh, yeah," said Jordan. "Like your tutoring girl called and said she got into some school or something."

Bret swung his head up to look at him, eyes wide. "She did," he asked.

"Yeah," said Jordan. "Something like that."

Bret picked up the red cup and drank. A few big swallows he couldn't even taste.

There in the doorway Masters stood waiting with a gentle smile, and Bret went to him unresisting.

Amanda from Alpha Phi leaned against the wall. Some dude had spilled beer all over her pale pink top, and some dude was talking to her and grabbing her ass. She bit her pinkie, deep in thought, trying to figure out if it was the same dude.

She heard a voice say, "Whoa, let's move back here. Coming through." The bodies packed in front of her seemed to be separating a little.

A guy came stumbling through, more falling forward than actually walking. He bumped into people who either didn't notice or pretended not to care.

Oh, it was that cute guy from *Spring Break Undercover*! He looked really wasted. God, what was his name again?

He had his arm around another guy, Sam Masters, who she remembered because he was PAK House President and she had to memorize them all like two weeks ago. Masters was holding him up and steering him through the crowd.

Okay, she was definitely getting an ass squeeze from the *same dude* who had spilled beer on her. Now all she had to do was figure out if that was okay or not.

The really drunk guy from *Spring Break* had dull eyes and he almost fell into her. She shrank away instinctively, but Masters reeled him in and plunged him back into the crowds.

As they passed, she heard Masters saying the following strange thing: "It doesn't *mean* anything, bro. It's a fucking necklace."

He moved aside some guy who was doing a little dance in their path. Then he went on: "And, uh, dude, I keep telling you that thing's just weird. I got this sweet shell one I'll give you instead. Birthday present."

And the really drunk guy said, "Okay."

And then they disappeared.

Amanda reached a decision: It was *so uncool* that this dude was grabbing her ass after spilling beer on her top. Now, what should she do?

21

Babble and nausea filled all beyond a distant wail of sirens. Masters rose out of the roaring vortex surrounded by dawn light. Solid, reassuring, steady against the throbbing beat, he pressed a slender crystalline shot glass into Bret's open hand. Something clear, maybe vodka.

"You're at twenty, bro," Masters breathed. *"Be twenty-one."*

Bret looked at the glass and tried to focus. Before the lifting sun, he inhaled and smiled. "'Fire renews everything,'" he said.

Masters nodded proudly, slapped him on the back, shot him the point with two index fingers. "All eyes are on you," he lied.

o   o   o

Bret's world was light and dark, sounds that rose and fell. He lay helplessly in protective arms and felt surrounding warmth and the steady pulse of heartbeat.

Everyone was watching him. The only face he could dimly see was his mother's, looking down tenderly as she cradled him in secret bond. But his father stood beside her, arm on her shoulder. His grandparents were there too, and his aunt Dorothy next to them, clay under her fingernails.

The room was white. Light streamed in the window. Flowers and cards clustered on the sill. One had a picture of a sun on it.

Bret knew light and dark, heartbeat and warmth, rising and falling sound.

He was monitored closely, but there were no surprises. Everything was so peaceful here at the beginning. Or the end.

About the Author

Jeremy Iversen is a recent graduate of Stanford University, where he was vice president of his fraternity. He lives and writes in Southern California. This is his debut novel.

the party room

by Morgan Burke

The party room is where all the prep school kids drink up and hook up. All you need is a fake ID and your best Juicy Couture to get in.

One night, Samantha Byrne leaves with some guy no one's ever seen before . . . and ends up dead in Central Park. Murdered gruesomely. Found at the scene of the crime: a school tie from Talcott Prep.

New York is suddenly in the grip of a raging media frenzy. And a serial killer walks amidst Manhattan's most privileged—and indulged—teens.

And the party isn't over yet. . . .
Last Call in June 2005!

Published by Simon Pulse

As many as 1 in 3 Americans
who have HIV... don't know it.

TAKE CONTROL.
KNOW YOUR STATUS.
GET TESTED.

To learn more about HIV testing,
or get a free guide to HIV and
other sexually transmitted diseases:

www.knowhivaids.org
1-866-344-KNOW